1

W

by:
Leighann Dobbs

This book is dedicated to my fans. Without their support, it would never have been written.

This is a work of fiction.

None of it is real. All names, places, and events are products of the author's imagination. Any resemblance to real names, places, or events are purely coincidental, and should not be construed as being real.

Cover art by: http://www.coverkicks.com

Other Works By Leighann Dobbs

Lexy Baker
Cozy Mystery Series
* * *

Killer Cupcakes
Dying For Danish
Murder, Money & Marzipan
3 Bodies and a Biscotti
Bodies, Brownies & Bad Guys
Bake, Battle & Roll

Blackmoore Sisters
Cozy Mystery Series
* * *

Dead Wrong
Dead & Buried
Dead Tide

Contemporary
Romance
* * *

Reluctant Romance
Sweet Escapes - 4 Romance stories in one book

Dobbs "Fancytales"
Regency Romance Fairytales Series
* * *

Something In Red
Snow White and the Seven Rogues
Dancing on Glass
The Beast of Edenmaine

Table Of Contents

Chapter One

Lexy Baker smoothed the material of her silk wedding gown over her slim hips and smiled at her reflection in the three-sided mirror. Her shoulder length brown hair piled on top of her head accentuated her high cheekbones and highlighted her green eyes. She'd tried several different hairdos and finally decided this was the style she wanted for her wedding.

She turned first left and then right to check out the fit from every angle. Squinting at the mirror, she wondered if the gown was too small on top. She grabbed it from the top and hefted it upwards to cover her breasts a little better.

Was the gown too revealing?

She certainly hoped not. Her wedding to hunky police detective Jack Perillo was less than a week away and she didn't have time to get fitted for a new one. Besides, this was her dream gown, exactly what she'd pictured since she was a little girl. She'd had it specially made and it fit her like a glove, giving her a sophisticated air with just enough sparkle.

The rhinestones on the top of her gown reflected dazzling light like they were plugged in with miniature light-bulbs inside. Her brow creased slightly as she looked down—she didn't remember the gown being quite so sparkly before.

Glancing up, she realized that the brilliance of the stones were magnified by the opulent chandelier dangling from the twenty-foot ceiling in the bridal showroom at *Chez Philippe*—home of world renowned gown designer Philippe Montague.

In the mirror, she could see her grandmother Mona Baker, or Nans as Lexy called her, seated on the white tufted sofa right behind her. Beside Nans, Lexy's best friend, Cassie, smiled and gave her a thumbs-up as she munched on a chocolate chip cookie from Lexy's bakery, *The Cup and Cake*.

"Do you guys like it?" Lexy asked them over her shoulder.

"It's gorgeous dear," Nans said, nibbling noisily on a pistachio biscotti.

Lexy looked down at her chest. "You don't think it shows too much up top, do you?"

"Nah." Cassie shook her head, the red tips of her blonde spiked hairdo moving back and forth like the crest of a bird. "Not any more than any of the other gowns here." She gestured to indicate the large room filled with brides and gowns.

Lexy's gaze drifted to the showroom behind her with its theme of sparkle on white. White rugs, white overstuffed couches, white walls, white wedding gowns loaded with satin and lace hanging on racks around the room and thrown over chairs. The room was aglow with crystal accents, the lights reflecting in the dozens of mirrors, each with a bride in front of them doing exactly what Lexy was doing.

Her heart jolted when she saw a familiar pair of eyes looking at her from a mirror on the other side of the room. Dark, cold, beady eyes.

It couldn't be.

Lexy and the other bride spun around at the same time. They stood on opposite sides of the room, glaring at each other. Lexy sucked in a breath, her good mood plummeting as her eyes verified the other bride was exactly who she'd thought—Veronica Maynard—her nemesis from high school.

Veronica hated Lexy back then. Lexy had no idea why. Sure, Lexy was prettier, got better grades and the boys seemed to like her better. But that was no reason to hate a girl, was it?

Veronica had delighted in taunting her, stealing her lunches, her boyfriends and playing tricks on her. Like pouring honey on her locker handle and cutting the seam of her gym shorts. Judging by the way Veronica was stomping across the room, her feelings toward Lexy hadn't changed.

"You!" Veronica screwed up her face and jabbed her index finger at Lexy.

"Hello, Veronica." Lexy eyed Veronica's poufed-up hairdo which was corralled in place with a glittering tiara. Not much different from her high school hairdo ... except for the tiara.

Lexy heard Cassie suck in a breath from her seat on the sofa. Cassie and Lexy had been best friends in high school and shared the same dislike for Veronica.

"How *dare* you wear the same dress as mine!" Veronica wavered her finger around Lexy's body.

Lexy looked down at her gown, then over at Veronica's. They *were* similar. Very similar. Almost identical, she realized with a start.

"Take it off," Veronica demanded.

Nans shot up from her place on the couch. "Now, see here, Bridezilla." Drawing herself to her full five-foot-two height, she marched over to Veronica and stabbed her finger in the other girl's face. "You can't bully my granddaughter like that. Back off or you'll have *me* to answer to."

Veronica shot Nans a sideways glare as she stomped closer. Lexy squared her hips, her hands curling into fists at her sides.

"Listen Maynard," Lexy said. "You might have been able to intimidate me in high school, but we're all grown up now. I'm keeping the dress."

Cassie threw down her cookie and stood beside Nans, shooting angry looks at Veronica.

"I had mine custom made," Veronica said.

"So did I." Lexy wondered if Veronica had somehow seen her dress design and copied it. It would be just like Veronica to try to copy Lexy—she'd often shown up at school with almost the exact same outfit days after Lexy had worn hers.

"My gown is supposed to be one of a kind." Veronica narrowed her eyes at Lexy.

"Wait ... someone is actually marrying you?" Cassie tilted her head at Veronica, her eyebrows raised.

Veronica threw her head back and the tiara threatened to tear her hair loose. "Yes *and* we're getting married in Paris."

"If you're getting married in Paris, what do you care if your gown looks like Lexy's? She's getting married here," Nans said.

"It's the principle. I paid for a custom design." Veronica slid her eyes over to Lexy. "And I look much better in it than *she* does."

Lexy's face flushed with anger and she opened her mouth to give Veronica a piece of her mind when a movement behind the other bride caught her eye. She peered around Veronica and her stomach tightened when she recognized another of her high school enemies—Ramona Kazlowski.

Back in high school, Ramona had followed Veronica like a baby duck. They did the same things, taunted the same classmates, wore similar clothes and even had the same hairstyle. Lexy was surprised to discover that now, more than fifteen years later, they still wore their black hair in an identical poufy style. She found herself wondering if they'd worn similar outfits to the fitting.

Ramona looked Lexy over.

"Yeah, you do look better, Ronnie. And what's with your boobs, Baker? They're practically falling out. Did you get a boob job?" Ramona thrust her chin at Lexy who looked down at her bust again.

Maybe it was *too tight?*

Lexy glanced over at Veronica's boobs, which seemed to be better proportioned to the confines of her gown.

"No. I didn't get a boob job," Lexy said. "Veronica's are just too small."

Cassie and Nans put their hands to their mouths to stifle twin giggles.

"What?" Veronica's face went red, she raised her voice. "Take that back!"

"I won't. It's true." Lexy raised her voice to the same level. Out of the corner of her eye, she noticed the rest of the brides had stopped their fittings and were turning to stare at them.

"Listen, you bitch, I'm not letting you ruin my special day by copying my gown. Give it to me." Veronica held out her hand as if she expected Lexy to just take off the gown and hand it over.

"What? No way. You copied me!" Lexy stood her ground.

Next to them, Nans, Cassie and Ramona's heads swiveled back and forth between the two arguing women.

"I said. Take it off." Veronica pushed Lexy's shoulder.

"Don't push me." Lexy pushed Veronica back, but much harder. Veronica stumbled backwards half a step and then regained her footing, rushing toward Lexy and pushing her with both hands this time.

Lexy's eyes went wide and she reached out to grab at Veronica. Both girls lost their footing and they ended up in a tangle of satin, lace and netting on the floor.

"Get off me!" Veronica scratched Lexy's arm.

"Ouch. That hurt!" Lexy pulled Veronica's hair and the left side tumbled out of its configuration.

Veronica let out a yowl and ripped the side of Lexy's gown.

"Hey, you ripped my dress!" Lexy yanked on the bodice of Veronica's gown, tearing it at the seam.

Lexy and Veronica tumbled around on the floor, each yelling expletives while trying to get in a punch. Out of the corner of her eye, Lexy could see Cassie and Ramona getting ready to jump in. Even Nans was starting to roll up her sleeves. The other brides were staring at them wide-eyed. Behind them, Philippe Montague ran in their direction waving his arms frantically.

"Ladies, Ladies. Please!" He bent down, trying to separate them. "I beg of you."

Lexy stopped fighting. She flushed with embarrassment—rolling around on the floor in a catfight wasn't anything grown women should be doing. Veronica must have realized how ridiculous they looked too and she rolled away from Lexy. The two women struggled to get to their feet, encumbered by their voluminous gowns.

Philippe stepped in between them, his forehead creasing as he looked them up and down. His face fell. "You have ruined my beautiful gowns."

Lexy looked down at her gown. Her stomach sank when she saw a big rip on the side and another down the front. *Would they be able to repair it in time for her wedding?*

"Hey, buddy. We have almost the same exact dress. What's up with that? I paid for a custom dress." Veronica held her gown to her chest to keep it from falling off as she turned her venomous stare on Philippe.

"What?" Philippe frowned as he looked from one gown to the other. "They are rather similar. You ladies must have given us similar instructions. And now they both need major repairs. You must take them off so Millie can work on them right away."

Veronica backed away, still holding her dress up.

"No way, pal. If you think I'm going to stand around and let you fix *her* dress so she can have the same gown as me, you've got another think coming!"

"But Madam—" Philippe sputtered then stopped as Veronica held up her hand cutting him off. She turned to glare at Lexy.

"You better start looking for another dress, Baker," she said holding her dress up with one hand and jabbing her finger at Lexy with the other. "Because I'm going to make sure you don't wear *that* one ... if it's the last thing I do!"

Chapter Two

Lexy's stomach sank as she stared at the wedding dress that lay folded on her couch. Angry over what had happened at the dress shop, she'd refused Philippe's pleas for her to leave it for him to repair and insisted on taking it home.

But now she had no idea how she was going to get it fixed. The ceremony was in less than a week. She'd worked so hard for everything to be perfect ... and now her dream dress was ruined.

She leaned over, lifted the lid on the box of goodies and peered in. Two éclairs, five snickerdoodles and two cupcakes. The sound of the bakery box lid attracted the attention of her dog, Sprinkles, and within seconds, the white Shih-Tzu mix was on the couch beside her, staring up at her expectantly.

"Hey, Sprinkles." She stroked the dog's white fur. "An éclair seems like it would really hit the spot right now, don't you think?"

Sprinkles beat her tail against the back of the couch in agreement as Lexy picked out the confection. She broke off a teensy piece of pastry and fed it to the dog before biting into it herself. Giving her dress a sideways glance she hoped she'd still fit in it as her taste buds enjoyed the explosion of sweet, silky custard.

One little éclair wouldn't make the dress too tight, would it?

The shrill ring of the phone caught her attention. She rummaged in her purse, frowning at the display. *Chez Philippe.* Sinking back into the couch with a sigh, she pushed the talk button.

"Hello?"

"Miss Lexy? It's Philippe Montague."

"Yes, Philippe. What can I do for you?"

"Please, I must beg you to bring the dress in so we can repair it. I feel terrible about what happened with you and Miss Veronica. I wish you would give me a chance to make it better."

Lexy fingered the tear on the dress. She was reluctant to go back to *Chez Philippe*, but she'd been unable to find anyone else who could repair it on short notice and her wedding budget was stretched so thin already she didn't know if she could even afford to pay anyone to do it.

Sensing her hesitation, Philippe said, "Miss Veronica has already agreed to meet here tonight."

Lexy's anger started to simmer at the mention of the other bride.

"Well, I have no intention of going anywhere near any place where *she* is," she said stiffly into the phone.

"No, no, Miss Lexy. I will meet with her separately. I will not subject you to her ... how do you say ... intimidations?" Lexy melted a little at Philippe's voice, which sounded full of apologies. His next words clinched it. "And, of course, the repairs will be free of charge."

"Free? Really? Great. What time do you want to meet?"

***

A niggle of doubt pulled at Lexy's stomach as she eyed the darkened interior of *Chez Philippe* through the glass door. Her appointment was at seven and, according to her phone, it was six fifty-eight.

A few minutes early, but shouldn't Philippe be here?

Then she remembered the main shop only stayed open until five—Philippe was probably in the back room and had left the lights off out front to discourage shoppers. She got out of her car with a shrug, grabbed her wedding dress from the back seat and clip-clopped up to the door in her tan suede Jimmy Choo's.

Opening the door, Lexy felt a shiver of premonition ... or maybe it was the air conditioning that seemed to be blasting on high. She hesitated in the doorway for a second, expecting Philippe to have heard the bell over the door and come out of the back to greet her.

A few seconds of silence ticked by before she proceeded further into the shop.

"Hello? Philippe?" She ventured.

Silence.

"Is anyone here?"

No one answered.

Maybe he is sewing in the back and can't hear me over the machines?

Lexy made her way across the salesroom floor toward the back of the shop. The mannequins, showing off the latest bridal gowns, which seemed fashionably welcoming in the light of day, suddenly leered at her with sinister intent.

Clutching her dress tighter to her chest, she picked up the pace.

"Mr. Montague ... it's Lexy Baker," she announced as she rounded the corner, then stopped short.

That's odd. The lights are off back here, too.

A familiar coppery metallic smell tickled Lexy's nose and the doubt that had pawed at her stomach earlier spread as she fumbled for the light switch. The lights came on and Lexy craned her neck to see around the sewing table, dreading what she might find.

Her heart jerked when she saw the bodies lying side by side on the floor. She threw her dress down on the table and ran over. She skidded in something wet and her stomach churned with the nauseating realization that it was a pool of spreading blood.

The back of her mind was screaming for her to run in the other direction, but she had to check if they were alive so that she could perform aid if necessary.

Why would someone kill Philippe and his assistant?

She reached Philippe first and checked for a pulse. Nothing.

She turned to the other body. From the doorway, she'd assumed it was Philippe's assistant who lay beside him but now, close up, she could see she'd been wrong. It was Veronica Maynard. And she was dead.

Why would someone want to kill Philippe and *Veronica?*

Lexy stood up, grabbed her dress off the counter and ran out to her car to call nine-one-one.

Chapter Three

Lexy's stomach churned as she heard the sirens getting closer and closer. It wasn't the site of the two bodies so much—she was getting kind of used to stumbling over dead bodies—but the arrival of her homicide detective fiancé that made her nervous. Jack had a tendency to get irritated with the way Lexy seemed to be a murder magnet, and with the wedding so close, she didn't want to rock the boat.

Two black and whites pulled to the curb along with an unmarked police car with Jack at the wheel and his partner, John Darling, riding shotgun. Lexy saw Jack's eyes narrow as he recognized her car, and she steeled herself with a deep breath.

Lexy got out and leaned against the car. Her top teeth worried her bottom lip as she watched Jack come toward her. She had to admit, his tall frame, broad shoulders and ruggedly handsome face still made her heart flutter. She just hoped he wouldn't be too mad.

"*You* called this in?" He raised a brow at her.

Lexy nodded.

"Two bodies?" He glanced back at the building where John was organizing the rest of the crew.

Lexy nodded again.

"Jeez, Lexy. Now you're finding them in batches." Jack shook his head and turned to start back across the street. Then he stopped, turned back toward her and took a step closer. He tucked a stray hair behind her ear, and her heart swelled when she saw the concern in his honey-brown eyes.

"Don't leave. We're going to need to question you." He brushed his lips quickly against her forehead then jogged back to *Chez Philippe,* disappearing through the front door and leaving Lexy to wonder what the heck had happened in there.

Lexy glanced into her car at her wedding dress, feeling selfishly happy that she hadn't left it in the store where it might be confiscated as evidence. The thought gave her a pang of guilt when she realized Veronica's dress might not be so lucky. Was it in there covered in blood? She couldn't remember what the room had looked like or what was in there, she'd been so focused on determining if either of them was alive. Either way, Veronica would never get the chance to wear it.

Suddenly stricken with an overwhelming curiosity, she stood on her tiptoes craning to see if she could make out what was going on inside. Jack probably wouldn't like it if she barged right in though, so she took out her phone and called Nans instead.

Not that long ago, Lexy discovered that Nans and three of her friends, Ida, Ruth and Helen, had an unusual hobby—they liked to solve murders. They were actually quite serious about it and even had a name for themselves—*The Ladies Detective Club*. That hobby had really come in handy when Lexy had been accused of poisoning her ex-boyfriend. Since then, the five of them had gone on to solve several other murders.

Lexy had to admit she had a fondness, and a bit of a talent, for solving murders ... even if Jack took a dim view of her extra-curricular activities. Nans would never forgive her if she found out Lexy had stumbled across more bodies and didn't call right away.

"Hello?" Nans answered the phone and Lexy could hear a din of conversation in the background.

"Hi Nans. It's Lexy."

"Oh. Hi, dear. I forgot to look at caller id again. How are you?"

"Good," Lexy said, "I have some interesting news."

"Hold on, dear."

Lexy could have sworn she heard someone yell "Bingo" before the sounds on the other end were muffled by Nans' hand covering the mouthpiece.

A few seconds later Nans came back on. “Sorry, dear. I had to go outside because I couldn’t hear.”

“Are you at Bingo again?” Lexy asked.

“Yes,” Nans said sheepishly. “Ida just won a hundred dollars—that’s a lot when you’re on a fixed budget with only social security checks to support you.”

“I’m sure it is.” A movement over in the store caught Lexy’s eye and she lowered her voice. “Never mind about that though, I have something exciting to tell you.”

“Oh? What?”

“Remember how I told you I was bringing my dress back to *Chez Philippe* tonight?”

“Yeeees.” Nans drew out the middle of the word.

“Well, you won’t believe what I found,” Lexy said.

“What?” Nans was starting to sound aggravated and Lexy could almost picture her making a circling gesture with her hand to indicate Lexy should move it along.

“Philippe Montague and Veronica Maynard.” Lexy paused for effect.

“In a compromising position?” Nans asked sounding much more interested.

“No. Dead.”

Nans gasped on the other end of the phone. "Did you say dead?"

"Yep."

"But who would want to kill them?" Nans asked.

"That's what I was wondering," Lexy said. "Jack's inside investigating the scene right now."

"What? And you're not in there?" Nans practically yelled into the phone.

"No. He told me to stay here." Lexy looked over at the doorway again. She really wanted to know what was going on in there.

"You need to get in there and listen to what they are saying. Find out what the clues are. Memorize the crime scene," Nans instructed. "Otherwise, how do you expect us to solve the murders?"

Lexy pressed her lips together trying to remember Jack's words. He hadn't actually said *not* to go in there, he'd just said not to leave. Which meant it was perfectly fine for her to go in.

"Okay, I'm going in. I'll call you later."

Lexy snapped the phone shut, walked over to the shop door, opened it and strode in like she belonged there.

***

No one questioned her entrance, so Lexy snuck into the back room and slid into a corner, wedging herself in between a dress form and the counter. The form was fully clothed in a hoop skirt wedding gown, which she hoped would hide her.

Jack was busy bending over the body with John and the medical examiner, Naomi Sprigs. Several crime scene investigators were busy taking pictures, dusting for prints and putting down yellow plastic cards with numbers on them. No one paid any attention to her.

She craned her neck to see what was going on over by the bodies. Naomi was pointing at different parts of the bodies, presumably the parts where the blood was coming out. With a start, Lexy realized she didn't even know what had killed them. She tilted her ear toward the trio, hoping to hear what they were saying.

"... gunshot wound here ... and here," Naomi said.

John stood up and walked to the back of the room. Lexy noticed there was a back door right behind him. He made a motion like he was holding a gun. Some of his words drifted over to Lexy.

" ... Killer ... stood ..."

From what she could gather, he was saying the killer must have come in the back door and stood where John was, firing the shots from there. So they were killed with a gun.

"Then, he probably ran back out." Jack's deep baritone carried over to Lexy.

Naomi stood up and pointed to something on the opposite side of the bodies. "Well, then, what about that?"

"And these." A crime scene tech pointed to several places on the floor leading out into the front room.

Lexy craned to see what she was pointing at. She cringed when she saw the smudged area of blood and subsequent footprints leading to the front, realizing it was she who had smudged the blood. Looking down at her shoe, she recoiled when she saw the smear of dark red on tan suede. Her elbow jerked out and hit the dress form, which teetered precariously before crashing loudly to the floor.

Everyone in the room jerked their heads in Lexy's direction making her feel like she'd been caught running naked down Main Street. Her cheeks burned and she managed a smile and finger wave.

"Lexy? What are you doing in here?" Jack's forehead pleated between dark masculine brows.

"Oh, I thought you said to stick around ..." Lexy plastered a look of innocence on her face.

Jack's eyes narrowed. "I think you knew I meant to stick around *outside*."

Jack's partner, John Darling stood behind Jack, his long ponytail cascading down the front of his leather jacket. He laughed good-naturedly and jabbed Jack in the arm.

"I think she's got you there, buddy," he said then turned to Lexy. "Hey Lexy, how's it going?"

"Good. You?" Lexy favored John with a genuine smile. Not only had she known the long-haired detective as long as she'd known Jack, but he was married to her best friend Cassie. She considered him a good friend.

"Never better," he replied. "I see you're up to your usual tricks of finding bodies."

Lexy cringed as she watched Jack and Naomi examine the bloody footsteps.

"Those look like high heels," Naomi said.

Jack cut his eyes to Lexy, then dropped them to her shoes. There was no mistaking the blood on one of them.

"When I saw the bodies, I rushed over to see if they were still alive." Lexy held her foot out. "I slid in the blood. Once I knew they were dead, I didn't want to sit in here with them so I ran outside to my car to call nine-one-one."

"We're going to have to take that shoe." Jack motioned to one of the crime scene investigators. "Take the shoe from Ms. Baker and bag it up as evidence. Check the other shoe too, if there's blood on it take—"

"Ackkkkk!"

His instructions were interrupted by a shriek in the doorway. Lexy jerked her head in the direction of the shriek just in time to see Millie, Montague's seamstress, drop a tray of Starbucks coffees on the floor, the lids popped off and the brown liquid was spreading toward the crime scene.

"Dammit, don't let that contaminate the crime scene!" Jack yelled. "Why isn't that front room secured?"

Someone scurried to clean up the coffee mess and a uniformed officer from the front room poked his head in. "Sorry, detective. The room is secure ... she came in through a side door."

Millie's hands flew up to her cheeks and she stood frozen in the doorway staring at the bloody mess.

Lexy saw Jack suck in a deep breath. "Okay, take her out front and find her a place to sit. I'll be out to talk to her in a minute."

Jack turned back to the bodies and Lexy took off her shoe and handed it to the CSI, then lifted the other shoe for his inspection. That one turned up clean so she didn't have to hand it over, but her stomach tightened when she saw her expensive Jimmy Choo in the evidence bag. Would she ever get it back?

Out of the corner of her eye, Lexy saw Jack heading out into the front room and she slipped into the room behind him. Hobbling off-kilter with only one shoe, she was careful to stay out of his direct line of sight but close enough so she could hear the interrogation.

Millie was seated on a white tufted bench—the same bench Lexy had sat on during her first visit. To her left was a rack of wedding gowns. Jack pulled a chair up opposite her and leaned toward her. Lexy could see the older woman was visibly shaken.

"Are you okay to answer some questions?" he asked in a soothing, low voice.

Millie nodded, dabbing at the corner of her eye with a tissue she'd pulled from the table beside her.

"Okay," Jack said as he pulled out a small spiral bound notebook. "What's your name and relation to Mr. Montague?"

"I'm Millie Townsend, Mr. Montague's seamstress." She sniffed.

"How long have you worked for Montague?"

Millie pressed her lips together. "Oh, well, I'd say at least twenty years."

Jack scribbled in the pad. "Do you know of anyone that would want to kill him?"

"Lordy no!" Millie blanched. "Everyone loved Philippe. He was a nice man."

"And what are you doing here ... at night?"

"I came in for some extra work. Mr. Montague was meeting with some clients that needed dress alterations."

"Does he meet with clients at night often?"

Millie fretted with the tissue in her hand, looking down instead of at Jack. "No, but there was an ... ummm ... altercation this afternoon and he set up special meetings because of that."

"An altercation?" Jack straightened in his chair.

"Yes. Veronica Maynard ... I believe that's who is in *there*." Millie pointed her chin toward the back room and tears spilled out of her eyes. Jack gave her a few seconds to compose herself as he scribbled in his notepad.

"Did Mr. Montague have an altercation with Ms. Maynard?" Jack asked.

"Goodness no! The altercation was between Ms. Maynard and another bride."

"Oh really?" Jack's voice was piqued with interest, causing a sinking sensation in Lexy's chest. "What was the fight about?"

Millie blushed. "Well, I really don't eavesdrop—you could hear them yelling all the way in the back room, though. But I only heard the tail end of the fight. If I'd known what was going to happen, I might have taken it more seriously."

"Why is that?" Jack asked.

"Because I heard Ms. Veronica say she'd stop the other bride from wearing the dress if it was the *last thing* she did."

Lexy could practically see Jack's ears perk up and she started to back slowly out of the room. Jack leaned closer to Millie and put his hand over hers.

"Now, think carefully Millie. Do you know who the other bride was?"

"Why sure," Millie said. Lexy's blood froze as the older woman pointed her index finger in Lexy's direction.

"She's standing right over there."

Chapter Four

Lexy hobbled down the hall of the police station, propelled along at twice her normal speed by Jack's vise-like grip on her elbow. Her uneven one-shoed gait made it hard for her to keep up, but she didn't have much choice.

He ripped open the door to an interrogation room and shoved her inside where she collapsed in the chair, exhausted.

Her heart sank as she watched him pace back and forth in front of the door. He stopped and faced her, hands on hips.

"It might have been nice if you'd mentioned that you had a fight with the deceased *and* your shoe was covered in her blood when I first got to the store," he said.

Lexy bit her bottom lip to ward off the tears that threatened to spill out of her eyes. "I know. I'm sorry. Honestly, I wasn't thinking straight—I didn't realize the fight we had earlier would be pertinent and I was too shocked at finding the bodies to even think about my shoe."

Jack's face softened. "I know. I don't mean to be harsh on you but I don't want it to seem like you were hiding that. Some might consider that suspicious."

The door to the room opened and John Darling slipped in, the plastic evidence bag with Lexy's shoe in his hand. "Are you guys ready?"

Jack pulled out a chair on the opposite side of the table from Lexy and sat down. "Sure. It's probably best if you ask the questions."

John nodded and sat in the chair next to Jack. He put the plastic bag on the table. Lexy's stomach fluttered nervously—she wasn't used to being questioned as a suspect, although having Jack and John do the questioning did make it less scary.

"Is this your shoe?" John pointed to the shoe in the bag.

"Yes."

"Why were you at *Chez Philippe* tonight?" John asked leaning back in his chair.

"I had an appointment with Philippe about my dress," Lexy answered.

"And what happened when you got there?"

Lexy thought back to earlier in the evening, trying to remember the details so she could explain them properly. "When I pulled up out front, the store was dark. I thought that was kind of strange, but since the store actually closes at five, I figured Philippe might be in the back. So I—"

The door to the room jerked open and they all looked up to see the Chief of Detectives, Willard Eames—Jack and John's boss.

"Hold it." Eames held his palm up toward them as he leaned against the door jam, the door still open.

Lexy squinted at the tall, thin man taking in his blue suit coat and red and blue diagonally striped tie. He had a sour look on his face, like someone had forgotten to put sugar in his lemonade.

"Huh?" John said.

"Aren't you Perillo's fiancée?" Eames said to Lexy.

"Yes."

"Then I think this could be a conflict of interest." Eames turned to Jack. "Perillo, you're off the case."

"What?" Jack stared at Eames, his eyebrows dipping into an angry V in the middle.

"Come on Jack, you know we're under scrutiny by internal affairs. I can't take any chances with one of my detectives being related to someone involved in the case," Eames said.

"But Lexy's not really *involved*," Jack said.

Eames' eyebrows lifted a fraction of an inch. "No? She found the bodies and has blood on her shoe. I think it's better for everyone if I put you and Darling on another case."

"But who will work this one?" Jack asked.

Eames smiled. "It just so happens we have someone who just passed the detectives' exam."

"We do? Who?" John asked.

"Watson Davies," Eames answered.

"A rookie?" Jack looked at Eames incredulously. "You're going to put a rookie on a double homicide?"

"Davies will be the lead detective, but you can still consult on the case," Eames said. "I just don't want either of you taking an active role."

Lexy felt panic clutch at her as she ping-ponged her head between the three men. Clearly, this Watson Davies wasn't anyone Jack trusted to do a good job ... and now that she was sitting in the interrogation room, she felt like it would be in her best interest that the detective on this case *did* a good job.

Jack sighed and stood up. "Okay, so where the hell is Davies then? We have a witness here for questioning."

Yeah, Lexy thought*; where the hell is Davies?*

Lexy heard a hollow clip-clop in the hallway and Eames half turned in that direction. A petite young blonde holding a manila folder full of papers appeared at his side. She wore a tattered jean jacket over a gray BRFPD tee shirt, a pair of faded jeans with holes in the knees and three-inch tall platform shoes, which were apparently the source of the clip-clopping. With the way she was chomping on a big wad of gum, Lexy figured her for a high school student—probably an intern.

Eames crossed his arms against his chest. "Davies, how nice of you to join us. Are those the case notes?"

Lexy's eyes widened ... *this* was Davies?

She looked like a kid. How could he possibly expect a rookie to handle something as complicated as a murder case? Lexy exchanged a panicked look with Jack and he put his hand over hers.

"Don't worry, everything will turn out okay," he reassured her.

"Of course it will. Davies here can handle everything just fine," Eames said and then looked pointedly at Davies. "Right, Davies?"

Lexy watched in amazement as Davies blew a gigantic pink bubble with her gum. It popped with a snap then she sucked the overflow back into her mouth.

"Are you kidding? This one is gonna be a piece of cake." She waved the file she had in her hand around in front of her. "According to this, the suspect had a violent argument with the victim, then later on she was found at the scene of the crime with the victim's blood all over her. I'd say this one's a slam dunk."

Davies shoved her way past Eames and tossed the file on the table.

"In fact, I can probably close this case tonight." She put her palms on the table and leaned toward Lexy, her baby blue eyes glinting like the cold steel of a switchblade. "Because it's obvious to me we have our killer sitting right here."

Chapter Five

Lexy rang the buzzer for Nans' apartment at the *Brooke Ridge Retirement Center* and leaned against the wall while she waited for her grandmother to buzz her in. She was exhausted from the night before when Davies had kept her at the police station for hours, drilling her with a battery of inane questions. The blonde detective seemed convinced Lexy was the killer and was obviously disappointed when Eames had to tell her to let Lexy go, as they had no real evidence to hold her on.

Lexy needed a pick-me-up this morning before she opened her bakery, and Nans' extra strong coffee was just the thing. Plus she knew that Nans and The Ladies Detective Club would be dying to hear all the details ... and judging by Davies fervor to pin the murders on her, Lexy figured she was going to need their help to find the real killer.

A garbled voice, which Lexy assumed was Nans, muttered gibberish over the intercom and Lexy pressed the button to talk.

"Nans? It's Lexy."

Lexy was sure the voices coming over the intercom on Nans' end were just as distorted, but her grandmother was expecting her and the door buzzed and clicked open.

Lexy pulled on the heavy glass door and made her way down the hall, the carpet muffling her footsteps. As she navigated the building to Nans' apartment, she could smell the intoxicating aroma of bacon and home fries. Her stomach grumbled and she hoped that Nans had a little box of pastries to go with her coffee.

She reached Nans door, her heart skipping when the door was jerked open before she even got the chance to knock.

"Good morning, dear." Nans shoved a mug of thick black brew into her hand and propelled her into the apartment.

Ruth, Ida and Helen were seated at Nans' mahogany dining room table, their heads turned in Lexy's direction, their eyes sparkling with excitement. A white bakery box in the middle of the table caught Lexy's attention and she walked over for a better look.

"Have a seat, dear," Ida said pulling out the chair next to her. Lexy sat and Ruth slid the pastry box over in front of her. Lexy picked a raspberry scone out of the box and Helen handed her a white embossed paper napkin to put it on.

The four ladies watched patiently as she settled back in her chair, took a bite of the scone and then washed it down with some coffee.

"So, tell us about the murders," Nans said. The other three women leaned in closer.

Lexy took another sip, closing her eyes as the caffeine started to do its job.

"Nans told you all about the fight at the dress fitting?" Lexy asked Ruth, Ida and Helen who all nodded their heads.

"Well, after that I went home, mad. My dress was ripped but I didn't want to go back to *Chez Philippe*. I made a few calls but no one could repair it on short notice. So, when Philippe called and begged me to come back saying he would fix the dress for free, I jumped at it."

Lexy paused long enough to take another bite of the sugary scone.

"And you went there and found the bodies," Ida prompted.

"Right. At first I thought no one was there, the store in the front was dark. But the door was open so I went in to look for Philippe in the back."

Ruth picked a gooey cinnamon bun out of the bakery box and put it on her napkin. "Why would you want to meet with this Veronica person?"

"I didn't," Lexy said. "He said he would meet with us separately, so I guess he was meeting with her first."

Nans pursed her lips. "So the killer might have been after either one of them, but not necessarily both of them."

"Right," Ida said as she nibbled on a lemon biscotti. "The other person might have just been in the wrong place at the wrong time."

"But why would anyone want to kill either of them?" Lexy asked.

"Well, that's what we need to figure out," Ruth said as she leaned over to rummage in her gigantic beige patent leather purse. A few seconds later, she came up with an iPad and placed it on the table in front of her. "Now, tell us who you think would have motive to kill them."

Lexy scrunched her face. "Me? I have no idea who would want to kill them—I don't even know them."

"Well you knew Veronica from school. Can you think of any enemies she had then?" Nans asked.

"Yeah, lots of people ... including me," Lexy answered.

"And you did have a knock-down drag-out fight with her that was witnessed by a room full of people the day she was murdered." Ruth wiggled her eyebrows at Lexy and the other ladies laughed. Lexy didn't find it so funny—no wonder Davies wanted to pin it on her.

"Well, we know Lexy didn't do it," Nans said. "So now we need to figure out who did. And you guys know where the best place to start is."

"The spouse!" Ida punctuated her words by crunching into the biscotti loudly.

"That's usually who it is. Probably one of them was having an affair and the spouse found out and killed him ... or her." Helen took a noisy slurp of tea from the bone china cup she held in her hand. "Happens all the time."

Ruth screwed her face up. "Yeah, but which one of them was having the affair."

Ida's face lit up. "Maybe they were having an affair with each other!"

"I don't think Philippe was married," Lexy said.

"We'll need to find that out," Ruth answered, as she typed into the iPad.

"Lexy, since you were a friend of Veronica, it's reasonable you would want to give your condolences to her fiancé," Ruth said.

Lexy's brow creased. "I don't know about that ... we hated each other."

"Oh, that was years ago." Helen waved her hand in the air. "You two are grown women now. Surely you could let bygones be bygones."

"I don't think so. We got into a fight just yesterday ..." Lexy shoved the last of the scone in her mouth.

"Well the fiancé doesn't need to know that. Besides it's really our only excuse to interrogate ... I mean *talk* ... to him," Nans said.

"And we need to find out about the murder weapon," Ida added.

"They were shot. I guess the killer came in the back door and shot them. At least that's what they said at the crime scene last night," Lexy said.

"Oh, well that helps. We need to find out what type of bullets they found and then find out if any of the suspects owned that kind of gun. Maybe Jack can help us with the details." Nans looked at Lexy.

"Well, that's the thing," Lexy said, "Jack's off the case."

The ladies gasped.

"What? Why?" Nans asked in obvious disappointment. Nans and Jack had a close relationship and the ladies often helped him on his cases. In turn, Jack would give them tidbits of information on cases they were trying to solve.

Without his 'inside' help, the ladies would have to work harder to find the killer.

Lexy sighed. "The chief of detectives said it wouldn't look good for him to be investigating given my involvement."

"So exactly *who* is on the case, then?" Ida asked.

Lexy's stomach sank. "Some new detective. It's her first case and she seems convinced I did it."

"All the more reason for us to find the real killer," Nans said. "Ruth, find out Veronica's fiancé's name and where he lives. Lexy, you meet me here at three p.m. on the dot. If we get lucky we could have the evidence we nccd bcforc supper tonight."

***

Lexy rushed across the parking lot to her car. Even though Cassie had worked as her assistant at the bakery since she opened it and was more than capable of running the place by herself, Lexy still felt guilty about leaving her there alone. She also had a dozen things to do today and needed to get the day's baking done early.

Her cell phone chirped in her pocket. She dug it out and glanced at the caller id, freezing in her tracks when she saw who it was. Her mother.

Lexy rolled her eyes as she hit "answer". She loved her mom, but the woman's exuberant enthusiasm could be overwhelming at times ... and Lexy had already used up most of her patience for the day.

"Hi Mom." Lexy warbled into the phone, trying to sound more chipper than she felt.

"Lexy!" Vera Baker's voice blared at high volume causing Lexy to hold the phone out six inches from her ear. "We're almost home, isn't that exciting?"

"Yes, Mom. I can't wait to see you and Dad." It was true, Lexy's parents had been traveling the country in an RV for over a year and Lexy *did* miss them.

"Me too. And we can't wait to meet your young man," Vera said. "Nans says such wonderful things about him."

Lexy's stomach fluttered. Her parents had never met Jack and she had a sudden case of nerves about whether the three of them would like each other.

"Are you sure we can park the RV in your driveway?" Vera asked.

"Yep, I'll just park my car on the street." Lexy grimaced, the gigantic RV would take up her whole driveway but she wanted to have her parents close by so she could spend more time with them.

"Okay, then. We should see you by supper time!"

"Great Mom. I can't wait!" Lexy said into the phone, but her mother had already hung up. She snapped the phone shut, her shoulders tight with stress. Her parents were making a special trip back to Brooke Ridge Falls for her wedding and while she *was* looking forward to their visit, it was going to be tough fitting them in when she also needed to run a bakery, finalize wedding plans and track down a killer.

Lexy shoved the phone in her pocket and sprinted for the car. She was going to have to work fast to check off all the items on the day's "to-do" list and still be able to meet Nans by three.

Chapter Six

It was three fifteen when Lexy pulled into the parking lot at the *Brooke Ridge Retirement Center*. Nans was already waiting for her just outside the door, her foot tapping impatiently on the pavement. Lexy pulled to a stop in front of her and motioned for her to get in.

"I was wondering if you were going to show," Nans said.

"Sorry, I got caught up in making lemon bars for the bakery."

Nans shrugged. "That's okay. You're here now so let's get down to business."

Lexy put the car in gear and swooped around the parking lot to get back to the entrance. "Which way?"

Nans pulled out her smartphone. "Let me get this navigation app up."

Lexy rolled down her window while Nans fiddled with the phone. The sky was a gorgeous shade of blue, the air crisp with the smell of fall and the temperature still warm enough to heat the car but not hot enough to require air conditioning. The open windows provided the perfect relief while letting in clean, fresh air.

"There," Nans said. "Take a left and then go through downtown and take a right on Howard Street."

Lexy checked the road for traffic then turned left.

"How did you find out where the fiancé lives?" Lexy was often baffled—and even a little disturbed—at how the ladies could dig up personal information.

"I knew Veronica's last name from the other day at the bridal shop, so Ruth just looked up her engagement announcement and we found the fiancé's name. Stuart Wiggins. Once we knew that, it was pretty easy to find out where he lives."

Lexy slid her eyes over to Nans. "And did you find out anything else about him?"

"Just that he's from Arizona and works as a security guard at the Telbourne Museum."

"Is that the big museum over in Cutler?" Cutler was a few towns over and a much larger city than Lexy's town of Brooke Ridge Falls. The museum was one of the largest in the world. Lexy frowned, remembering something about the museum in the news recently.

"Yep, that's the one. They had a recent theft ... some sort of crown jewels or scepter ... Howard is just up here on the right." Nans jabbed her finger at the right side of the windshield while looking down at her Smartphone.

Lexy turned right.

"Now follow this to ..." Nans squinted at the phone. "Palomino Lane, then take another left on Edwards. He lives in the townhouses somewhere on that road."

"Oh, I know just where that is," Lexy said.

"Great." Nans slipped the phone into her purse. "So your mom and dad are coming back tonight?"

"Yep. They said they'd be here at suppertime. You're coming over, right?" Lexy asked. Lexy's father was Nans' son, so she assumed her grandmother would want to join them.

"Of course, dear. We can head back once we get the evidence we need from the killer," Nans said with an air of confidence that Lexy wished she shared.

Lexy pulled up in front of the row of townhouses. They looked like any other townhouses—thin, two story homes stacked up next to each other, each in the same light blue siding with black shutters. Lexy shuddered when she realized one of them might harbor a killer.

Nans pushed her door open and jumped out, her face glowing with excitement. Lexy followed her onto the sidewalk.

"It's number forty-eight." Nans pointed to one of the middle townhouses and they started toward it.

"Looks like he didn't get his mail." Lexy pointed to the overstuffed mailbox on the side of the door.

"Or his paper," Nans said as the stood in front of the door looking down at a rolled up newspaper.

Lexy pressed the doorbell and waited.

No one answered.

"Maybe he's still at work. It is only three thirty," Lexy offered.

"Nope. He works the night shift." Nans looked at her watch. "Actually he should be just getting ready to *go* to work."

"Well, maybe he left early to run errands or something." Lexy backed down the walk to the one car garage. She went around to the side door. Standing on her tiptoes she cupped her hands around her eyes and looked in through the glass window. No car.

Lexy's spirits deflated. "Looks like he's not home." She came back around to the front only to find that Nans was no longer at Stuart's door. She was marching over to the next townhouse whose owner had the unfortunate timing to be out watering the plants next to his steps.

"Yoo-hoo." Nans waved at the elderly man who straightened from his task and contemplated Nans from underneath a bushy creased brow. "Sorry ... we were looking for Stuart Wiggins. You wouldn't happen to know where he is, would you?"

The man shrugged. "I don't know too much about him. Who are you?"

"Oh, I'm his great aunt ... just in town for a quick visit. I was hoping I could catch him." Lexy narrowed her eyes at Nans, feeling a little disturbed at how easily the other woman could spin off a lie.

"Oh. Well, I haven't seen him since yesterday." The man pursed his lips and looked up at the sky. "Come to think of it I didn't actually *see* him, but I heard him yelling."

"Yelling?" Nans asked.

"Yes. Must have been him and his lady friend having a fight. You know how young couples are." He winked at Nans.

"What were they yelling about?" Nans asked.

"Oh ... well I really don't like to talk out of school. Thing is, I couldn't make out everything they were saying. Something about lying I think." He shrugged. "Then I heard car doors slamming and looked out just in time to see that brunette peel out in a red Toyota Corolla, then saw Stuart come speeding out of his garage after her."

"Oh, well thank you," Nans said to the man, then turned and glanced triumphantly at Lexy. She hurried down the walkway, grabbing Lexy by the elbow and practically running to the sidewalk.

"This is great news," Nans whispered. "They got into a big fight, Veronica is found murdered hours later and the fiancé seems to be on the run—it's practically a written confession!"

They were almost to Lexy's car when a black sedan pulled to the curb. Lexy's heart twisted when Watson Davies jumped out of the driver's seat and approached them.

"What are *you* doing here?" Davies folded her arms against her chest and then stood there snapping her gum and looking from Lexy to Nans.

"Umm ... Nans, this is Detective Watson Davies." Lexy stalled. "Detective Davies, this is my grandmother, Mona Baker."

"Nans plastered a sugar sweet smile on her face. "It's sooo nice to meet you Detective Davies. Lexy has told me so many good things about you."

Davies lifted a perfectly plucked brow at Lexy.

"We were just here visiting an old friend of mine." Nans rushed on, waving to the man who had continued with his watering. "He's been cooped up inside for months and just now getting out. Isn't that wonderful?"

Davies looked uncertainly at the man, then narrowed her eyes at Nans. "You don't say."

"Yes, I do." Nans sprinted over to the passenger side of Lexy's car. "And now if you'll excuse us I'm late for a doctor's appointment!"

Nans jumped in the car and Davies fixed her attention on Lexy. "You don't expect me to believe that do you?"

Lexy's stomach churned and she crossed her fingers behind her back—she wasn't as accomplished a liar as her grandmother. "Are you accusing my grandmother of lying?"

Davies glanced at the car where Nans was fiddling with her Smartphone in the front seat.

"I don't know what you are up to, or how you got your grandmother involved, but I think you know full well Veronica's fiancé lives here. In fact, this makes me think maybe the two of you were in on the murder together."

"What? I don't even know him!"

"So you say," Davies said as she started toward Wiggins' townhouse. "But finding you here has just moved you up a notch on my suspect list."

Chapter Seven

"Thanks for making your famous lasagna," Lexy said to Nans as she slipped the glass baking dish filled with layers of pasta, ricotta cheese, meat sauce and mozzarella into the oven.

"Well, it *is* your father's favorite," Nans said spreading garlic butter liberally on Italian bread.

"Woof!" Sprinkles sat on the floor next to Nans' chair, her eyes focused on the bread like it was the last food on earth.

"You want a little piece?" Nans broke off a teeny piece of crust and held it out to the dog who spun in circles before gobbling down the morsel.

Lexy looked around the kitchen. The table was set, a bottle of wine was airing and the food was under control. A horn blasted in the driveway and Nans and Lexy exchanged a glance.

"Is that them?" Lexy ran to the front door, her eyes growing wide when she saw the forty-foot RV taking up most of her yard.

The door to the RV sprang open and her mother burst out. Vera Baker stood about five feet tall, was equipped with a bit of extra padding and was in perpetual motion. A shock of flame red hair framed her round face. As her mother ran toward her, Lexy noticed she looked tanned and happy—apparently, the nomadic RV life suited her.

"Lexy!" Vera practically knocked Lexy over with her usual enthusiasm.

"Hi, Mom. You look great!" Lexy held her mother at arm's length, warmth flooding her heart. Lexy and her mother didn't always see eye to eye, but the time apart had made Lexy realize how much she loved her.

Next to them, Nans and Lexy's father, Roy, were exchanging hugs and they traded off, giving Lexy a chance to greet her father.

"I missed my girl," he said as he hugged her gently. Roy Baker was the opposite of his wife. Tall and slim, he was calm, cool and collected. Lexy liked to think she took more after him than her overly enthusiastic mother.

Lexy stood back and looked at her parents. She noticed they were wearing matching Hawaiian shirts and wondered if she and Jack would ever end up wearing matching shirts. She certainly hoped not.

"Those shirts are cute," Nans said giving Lexy a look out of the corner of her eye that told her Nans thought they were anything but.

"Oh thanks." Vera bubbled. "I made them myself."

"You did? When did you start making clothes?" Lexy asked, surprised to learn about her mother's new hobby.

"Well, I had to find something to do to pass the time while Dad is driving the RV around, so I took up sewing."

"I have lots of custom made shirts now ... that I'm forced to wear." Roy winked at Lexy.

Vera wrinkled her brow as she scanned the yard. "When do we get to meet Jack?"

"Oh, he had to work tonight, but he'll be over tomorrow for breakfast," Lexy said, "If that's okay?"

"Sounds wonderful. I can make my famous cheese blintzes." Vera rubbed her hands together. "Now, let's get to the important stuff ... I want to see your dress."

Lexy's heart kicked. She didn't want to get into the whole Bridezilla thing with her mom. Especially not the part about how Bridezilla ended up murdered.

"Oh, it's inside ..." Lexy waved at the door, hoping her mother would sense she wasn't that keen on showing off the dress.

Vera whirled off in the direction of the front door. "Great. I want to see what you've done with the house too."

Lexy had bought the small bungalow from Nans a couple of years ago when Nans decided that living in the Retirement center would be more fun. It was the house her father had grown up in and the one that had given Lexy so many warm childhood memories. Not only that, but Jack lived in the house right behind hers which made dating really convenient.

Lexy's father shrugged and followed Vera into the house with Nans and Lexy trailing behind. Once inside, Lexy followed Vera around as she flitted from room to room commenting on the different things Lexy had done.

Once she'd inspected each room, Vera turned to Lexy, her hands clasped in front of her. "I can't wait anymore. Show us the dress. Do you want to model it for us?"

"Ahh ... well I can't exactly model it." Lexy chewed on her bottom lip.

"Why not?"

"It's not exactly finished."

"What? The wedding is in a few days—let me see it."

Lexy ran upstairs and grabbed the dress from her closet. It was probably best just to get it over with—when her mother had her mind set on something, it was impossible to dissuade her.

When Lexy came back down the stairs, she found everyone seated in the living room. They turned to look at her and she held the dress up in front of her.

Vera gasped. “Lexy, it’s gorgeous.”

Lexy’s heart swelled—it *was* gorgeous and exactly what she wanted, but would she be able to wear it? With Philippe dead, who would fix it for her?

Vera came closer, lifting the fabric and inspecting the rips. She bent down toward the gown and did some pulling and puckering while squinting and murmuring.

“I can fix this right up for you,” she said, straightening up and stepping back.

“You can?” Lexy asked, hope swelling in her chest.

“Of course. I’m quite good at sewing you know. I have a whole setup in the RV.” Vera reached her hand out for the dress and Lexy handed it over. “I’ll just take this to the RV after supper and have it fixed up for you in no time.”

Lexy felt the tension in her shoulders ease up. She hadn’t realized how stressed out she’d been about the dress. She reached over and hugged her mother.

“Thanks, Mom.”

The buzzer blared in the kitchen. "Oh that's the lasagna." Nans bolted up from the couch and bustled into the kitchen. Lexy, Vera and Roy followed with Sprinkles dancing at their heels.

Nans grabbed the salad and garlic bread and put them on the table while Lexy took the lasagna out of the oven, cutting it and dishing out big squares onto four plates. She put a little spoonful into Sprinkle's dish before joining everyone at the table.

"Oh this is delicious!" Vera gushed over her plate of food. "After supper you two can come and check out our RV. We'll show you our slideshow of all the places we've visited, like the world's biggest ball of twine, the largest hockey stick and the fifty-five foot tall Green Giant statue."

Nans raised her eyebrows and gave Lexy a look.

"Oh don't worry," Vera said catching the look. "It's only two hours long."

Lexy smiled at her mom as she bit into the gooey lasagna. Two hours of slides accompanied by her mothers' animated descriptions? She picked up her wine glass and drained the contents. She could hardly wait.

Chapter Eight

The next morning, Lexy glanced nervously out the kitchen window at Jack's back door while her mother busied herself at the counter mixing the ingredients for cheese blintzes. Her stomach flip-flopped when she saw Jack slip through the door and start across his backyard and into hers. She ran over to her kitchen door to open it for him feeling like a teenager about to introduce her parents to her prom date.

"Good morning." Jack's smile warmed his eyes and Lexy pushed the door open further beckoning him in.

Her father looked up from the crossword puzzle he'd been doing at the kitchen table and her mother, who was covered in flour by now, stopped mixing.

"Jack, I'd like you to meet my parents—Vera and Roy." Lexy motioned to each of her parents in turn and Jack shook hands with them.

"Nice to meet you both," Jack said then nodded at Vera's flour covered apron. "I see the apple doesn't fall too far from the tree."

Vera tittered. "Oh, I can see we're going to like you," she said pulling Jack over to the table. "Sit and I'll have these blintzes ready in a jiffy."

Jack did as he was told. Vera ran back to the counter and quickly poured the pancake-like batter into a hot pan, tipping the pan this way and that to cover the entire bottom. A few seconds of cooking and she flipped the pancake out and onto a sheet of waxed paper. Lexy plopped a generous dollop of the sweetened ricotta and cream cheese filling her mother had made earlier into the middle of the pancake, then folded it up like an envelope.

They repeated the process for three more blintzes then put them all into a large pan of hot oil, the addition of the blintzes making the oil snap and pop. The sweet smell of frying dough filled the air and a few minutes later the blintzes were a crisp golden brown. Vera lifted them out onto separate plates and Lexy added fresh strawberries on top.

Vera brought them to the table and plopped them in front of Jack and Roy, who had been mulling over the crossword puzzle together. Then she pushed Lexy down into one of the empty chairs and put a plate in front of her.

"Eat 'em while they're hot." Vera sank into the fourth chair and started in on her blintz.

Lexy cut off a small corner of the blintz as she watched Jack dig into his, cutting it open so the cheese filling oozed out and then scooping some of the pancake, filling and a strawberry onto his fork.

"This is delicious!" he said sliding his eyes toward Lexy. "How come you never made these for me?"

Lexy shrugged. "I could never make them as good as Mom."

"Oh pffft," Vera said as she scooted up from the table and busied herself cleaning off the counter. "So, Lexy told me a little about how you guys met. Is it true you almost arrested her?"

Jack laughed. "Well, I had a pretty good idea she wasn't the killer from the start. I just used that as an excuse to see more of her."

"Well I hardly think you need an excuse seeing as you live right in each other's back yard." Vera turned and winked at Lexy. "*That* must be convenient."

Lexy took a big gulp of water to try to extinguish the fire in her cheeks. It *was* convenient but the last people she needed thinking about that were her parents. Jack was apparently too busy finishing his blintz and then eating most of Lexy's to be embarrassed.

"So, it must be exciting to be a homicide detective," Vera said as she swept over to the table and took the plates away. Lexy had to fight to keep hers—she wasn't done yet.

"It's not as exciting as one might think—except for meeting beautiful women all the time." Jack winked at Lexy and her parents laughed.

"Are you working on any interesting cases now?" Roy asked.

Lexy's stomach twisted and she shook her head subtly hoping Jack would get the hint. She didn't need her parents getting wind of the murder at *Chez Philippe*.

"I'm not really on a case at the moment," Jack said and Lexy sagged with relief.

"It's so exciting you two are getting married," Vera said. "Jack, I know you'll be a great husband and you'll take good care of our little girl—Mona speaks so highly of you."

"Mona's a great gal," Jack said sincerely.

Jack had bought his house behind Lexy's when her grandmother still lived there and they'd been neighbors for a couple of years before Nans moved to the retirement center. In that time, Jack and Nans had become good friends while Jack did a lot of handy work on the house and Nans filled him with home-cooked meals. Jack had given Nans her interest in solving crimes—something Lexy was sure he regretted at times.

"Well, I hope we'll get to see a lot of you this week and get to know you better," Vera said as she swiped Lexy's plate with one hand and wiped the table with the other. She threw the plate in the dishwasher and the towel in the sink. "Come on Roy, I need you to put up some shelves in the RV."

Lexy's father rolled his eyes, picked up the paper with the crossword puzzle he was working on and stood, holding his hand out to Jack. "Nice to meet you."

Jack stood, meeting Roy's hand with his. "Same here."

"Nice meeting you Jack!" Vera yelled from the front door. "Come on Roy!"

Roy gave another eye roll, turned and left.

Lexy plucked at her napkin, suddenly very nervous. *What if Jack didn't like her parents?*

Jack reached over and pulled her onto his lap.

"You're parents are charming," he said nibbling on her ear.

Lexy swatted him away and tried to wiggle out of his lap but he held tight. She stayed in his lap casting nervous glances toward the door. With the way her mother operated, she could whirl back into the kitchen unannounced at any time. But she wanted to stay on Jack's good side ... she needed information from him.

"So, have you heard anything more about the double murder case?" Lexy asked.

“There was a break-in at *Chez Philippe* last night,” Jack said between nibbles.

Lexy pushed away to look at his face. “Really? That’s kind of strange isn’t it? Do you think it’s related to the murders?”

“Well, they were clearly looking for something because the place was ransacked. But if it was the murderer, why wouldn’t he have searched it when he was there doing the killing?” Jack asked taking a sudden interest in unbuttoning her shirt.

“Maybe he got interrupted and had to come back later.” *What if* she *was the one that had interrupted the killer?* Lexy felt a cold chill run up her spine thinking of how she might have been the third victim.

“And what about you?” Jack stopped the unbuttoning and studied her face. “I heard you had a run in with Detective Davies.”

Lexy’s stomach tightened. Jack didn’t like it when she got in the middle of on-going investigations but, in this case, she felt like she had a right to.

“Nans and I might have paid a little visit to Veronica’s fiancé.” She chewed her bottom lip and looked at Jack. “I know you don’t like it when we investigate, but I’m not that confident in Davies’ abilities. If it were *you* on the case I’d feel better, but right now I feel like investigating with Nans and the ladies is my best chance. You saw how hot Davies was to pin this on me."

"I know, and I agree with you," Jack said massaging the tension out of her shoulder.

"You do?"

"Yep."

"Great, then maybe if you find anything out like what type of gun they were killed with or any other evidence the police found, you could pass that along," she said. "But after what we found out yesterday, that might not be necessary, because I'm sure the police will soon find out the fiancé is the killer."

"Oh? What did you find?"

"Veronica and her fiancé had a big fight and they took off in separate cars right before the murder. The fiancé hasn't been home since," Lexy said. "Seems to me, if I were going to kill my fiancé, I'd high tail it out of town and get as far away as I could, too."

"Sure, that makes sense," Jack said. "But if the fiancé is the killer and he's on the run, who broke into *Chez Philippe*?"

Chapter Nine

Lexy didn't have time to think about who had broken into *Chez Philippe*—she had a lot to do at the bakery and still had to find time to meet with the wedding planner to finalize the menu.

She extricated herself from Jack's lap, pushed him out the back door, fed Sprinkles and then made a mad dash for her car stopping at her parents RV only long enough to bang on the door and yell a quick 'good-bye'. The sound of her father's power drill pierced the air as she pulled out of the driveway.

Fifteen minutes later, she was pulling into her spot behind the bakery. The smell of vanilla and sugar hit her as soon as she opened the door. She stood in the back entrance inhaling the intoxicating scent. There was nothing she loved more than the smell of fresh baked cookies.

Peeking into the kitchen, she could see Cassie at work folding chocolate chips into a large stainless steel bowl. Cassie looked up and smiled.

"I've been waiting for you!" Cassie threw down the bowl, ran over to the other side of the room and grabbed a brown box. "This came in the mail yesterday and I've been dying to show it to you."

Lexy didn't remember ordering anything. She walked over to the table as Cassie dug excitedly in the box, the smile growing on her face as she lifted out what was inside.

"I ordered it special for your cake." Lexy stared at the item that Cassie held triumphantly in her hand. It was a wedding cake topper, the bride with a chef's hat and the groom in a police uniform.

"What? I didn't even know you could order stuff like that." Lexy's heart swelled at the thoughtful gesture. "That was so nice of you." She turned and crushed Cassie in a hug.

"Well, you are my best friend ... and you did trust me to make the most important cake of your life."

Cassie had worked as Lexy's assistant since she'd opened the bakery and was becoming quite proficient in baking with a particular flair for cake decorating. When she'd offered to make Lexy's wedding cake, Lexy had happily accepted, she could think of no one better to trust the job to than her best friend.

"It's perfect," Lexy said.

"Well I figured you could use a pick me up after all that business over at *Chez Philippe*." Cassie put the topper gently back into the box.

Lexy rolled her eyes and leaned against the counter eyeing the plates of oversized cookies that were waiting to be displayed in the glass bakery cases out front. Her mouth watered and she thought about nibbling on a snickerdoodle until she remembered she'd just wolfed down most of a cheese blintz. Better to hold off on the cookies if she still wanted to fit into her gown.

"I know, I need that like I need a hole in the head ... I'm so busy with all this wedding stuff, when will I find time to investigate a double murder?"

"Yeah, John couldn't believe they put a rookie in charge." Cassie made a face.

"Tell me about it ... worst part is, she seems to be hell-bent on proving *I* did it. I would feel so much better if Jack and John were investigating it."

"At least you have Nans and the ladies, right?" Cassie crossed over to the oven, shoved her hands in oven mitts, took two cookie sheets out and deftly scraped the cookies onto racks to cool.

"Yeah, thankfully. Otherwise I might be looking forward to wearing handcuffs instead of a wedding ring," Lexy said. "Nans and I went over to talk to Veronica's fiancé yesterday and found out something that will hopefully clear me so I shouldn't have to worry about it anymore."

"Oh?" Cassie picked up two trays of cookies gesturing for Lexy to take the others. Lexy picked up the trays and told Cassie about the couple's fight and disappearance of the fiancé while the girls walked to the front of the store.

Cassie slid the door of one of the glass pastry cases open and leaned in to arrange the cookies. Lexy took a moment to look around the front room of her shop and her lips curled up in a smile. She'd always dreamed of owning her own bakery and a few years ago, thanks to a loan from her parents, her dream had come true.

Her bakery, *The Cup and Cak*e, was situated in an old mill building that sat in the middle of downtown Brooke Ridge Falls. In the back was the kitchen where she and Cassie did all the baking, and the front room had glass display cases full of pastries along with café tables that sat next to a floor-to-ceiling window with a picture perfect view of the falls the town was named for. A self-serve coffee station was setup near the tables and the pungent aroma of fresh brewed coffee spiced the air.

"Wait a minute, I thought John told me *Chez Philippe* got broken into last night," Cassie said looking back over her shoulder and interrupting Lexy's thoughts.

"Yeah, I know. I just found that out from Jack. I figured Stuart—her fiancé—would be halfway across the country by now." Lexy moved to the second pastry case and opened the door, reaching in to rearrange some of the items to fit the cookies.

"Maybe he broke back in to remove evidence or something," Cassie suggested.

Lexy frowned at the peanut butter cookies she was stacking in the case. "Maybe, but Jack said the place had been searched. You'd think the evidence would be right out in plain sight ... why would he have to search?"

"That's a good question." Cassie stacked the last of her cookies in the case and stood up, one giant chocolate chip cookie in her hand. "Maybe there was something in the store or their files he didn't want the police to find? Just where, exactly, did he search?"

Lexy finished with her display and stood up. "I don't know ... I'll have to ask Jack."

Cassie broke the cookie in half and handed half to Lexy. "Well in any event, it seems like the fiancé running away is a sure sign of his guilt, so that lets you off the hook."

"Yep." Lexy nibbled her half of the cookie. "I'm going to stop by the police station later today and get my shoe back."

"Your shoe?" Cassie wrinkled her forehead at Lexy.

"When I found the bodies I ran over to see if I needed to do CPR or something and I stepped in blood. They took one of my Jimmy Choo's as evidence."

"No wonder you want it back. Those things cost a mint."

"Yeah, I just hope I can clean it off." Lexy's stomach twisted. She didn't want to wear bloodstained shoes, but she'd splurged on that pair and her budget didn't allow for too many expensive shoe purchases. "Anyway, I'm sure detective Davies will have figured out the fiancé is the killer by now and will be willing to knock me off the suspect list."

"One can only hope. I heard she was kind of ditzy." Cassie shoved the last of her half of the cookie into her mouth.

"You might say that, but I feel pretty confident that even Watson Davies will agree the case is closed." Lexy nibbled on her cookie thoughtfully. "I mean, it's pretty obvious Stuart Wiggins is the killer—why would he have disappeared if he wasn't?"

Cassie shrugged. "Right, he would have no reason to run, so it makes sense to me that he did it."

"He probably killed her in a fit of anger. They had the fight. He chased her in the car and found her at *Chez Philippe*." Lexy frowned. "Poor Philippe just happened to be in the wrong place at the wrong time."

"That explains almost everything ... except the break-in," Cassie said.

Lexy sighed. "I know ... and I know exactly what Nans is going to say once she finds out about it."

"What's that?"

"If there's something in the store Stuart didn't want the police to find, then there may be more to this case than meets the eye."

Chapter Ten

It was mid-afternoon when Lexy pulled into the Brooke Ridge Falls Police Department parking lot. She'd finished the day's baking and left Cassie in charge at *The Cup and Cake*, then dropped the final guest list off at the wedding planner and reviewed the menu. Now she just had to get her shoe back and her day would be complete.

She felt pretty confident that she'd be welcome at the BRFPD because she'd brought her secret weapon—a box of goodies from the bakery.

Pushing open the double glass doors, she walked up to the desk.

"Help you?" the woman behind the chest high desk that separated the lobby from the inner workings of the station asked mechanically without even looking up. Lexy recognized her from previous visits to the station. The name on her uniform—Bristlecone—helped jog Lexy's memory.

Lexy slid the oversized box onto the counter "Hi, Officer Bristlecone. I was hoping I could talk to Detective Davies."

Bristlecone looked at the counter, her eyes lighting up when she saw Lexy ... or was it when she saw the pastry box? Either way, she seemed receptive to Lexy's request.

"Oh, hi Lexy. Let me see if she's in." Bristlecone stood up and peeked under the lid of the box.

"Please, help yourself. I brought them for everyone," Lexy said.

Bristlecone picked out a brownie, wrapped it in a napkin and stashed it under some papers on the corner of the desk. "Thanks. I'll go get Davies."

Lexy tapped a cherry red nail on the counter while she waited. There wasn't a lot of crime in her little town and the station was quiet. A few of the uniformed officers were sitting at metal desks in the squad room, busy with paperwork or phone calls. She knew from previous visits that the door on the left opened to the hallway that led to the regular offices and interrogation rooms. She'd been back there many times to visit Jack in his office and now wondered if Davies had her own office.

She didn't have to wait long to find out. The door opened and Davies appeared wearing skintight black jeans, and a black tee shirt with what looked like graffiti on it.

She snapped her gum at Lexy. "Ahh, Ms. Baker. Did you come to confess?"

Lexy frowned at the small blonde. "Hardly. In fact, I'm sure by now you have enough evidence on the fiancé ... or you should."

"Come on in so we can talk." Davies jerked her head toward the hall and held the door open.

Lexy grabbed the pastry box and followed her. Pastries always worked when she wanted information out of Jack and the other detectives. She didn't know if they would have the same effect on the disagreeable Davies, but it was worth a try.

Davies' shoes clickety-clacked on the beige industrial tile floor and Lexy studied them with envy. Black patent leather stilettos with steel spiked studs. Davies might not be the sharpest detective on the force but she sure did have good taste in shoes. Lexy wouldn't mind a pair of those herself and was debating the wisdom of having the same shoes as the detective when Davies stopped in front of one of the offices causing Lexy to almost knock her over.

Davies turned around and gave Lexy a mashed up face look. "Hey, do you mind?"

"Sorry, I didn't realize you were going to stop here."

Davies rolled her eyes, pushed the door open and gestured for Lexy to go in first. The room was large with four desks set up one behind the other. Lexy remembered that it served as an office for several people—only the higher-ranking detectives, like Jack, got their own office. Davies led her to the last desk and pulled a chair over for Lexy to sit in. The top of the desk was littered with papers, post it notes and a several bottles of nail polish. Lexy pushed the pastry box across the surface.

"So, tell me, what evidence should I have on the fiancé?" Davies sat with her elbows splayed on the desk, hands steepled in front of her, her chin resting on top of her fingers.

"Well, I assume you know he's missing," Lexy said.

"Yes, *I* know that, but how do *you* know that?"

Lexy felt a tingle of uneasiness. "Umm ... well he wasn't at home yesterday when I took my grandmother there ... to visit the neighbor."

"Right. I forgot you were visiting the *neighbor*." Davies flipped open the lid of the pastry box, took a sniff and then leaned back in her chair. "That's a pretty big coincidence that he happened to live next to Ms. Maynard's fiancé."

Lexy shrugged. "What does it matter? Surely you can see the fiancé disappearing after a big fight as a pretty big clue that he did it."

"Fight?" Davies left brow rose a fraction of an inch.

She didn't even know about the fight? Lexy wondered how much of Davies' job she'd have to do for her in order to get the case solved properly. "Yes, his neighbor heard Veronica and her fiancé—

Stuart—having a big fight the day she was murdered."

Davies sat up in her chair and grabbed a notepad. "What about?"

"I have no idea, but he said she drove off and Stuart peeled out after her," Lexy said. "So, I'm pretty sure that clears me and I was hoping I could get my shoe back."

"That suede Jimmy Choo? That's a nice shoe."

Lexy nodded.

Davies pulled out a piece of gum and shoved it into her mouth. "I'm not convinced about this. Plus, I think it's strange that you know so much—you might be the real killer lying to make it look like—"

The phone ringing on Davies desk interrupted her and she picked up the receiver.

"Davies," she barked into the phone.

She narrowed her eyes at Lexy. "And where did you find him?"

Davies scribbled something down on a piece of paper and Lexy fidgeted in her seat—she just wanted to get her shoe and get out of there.

"I'll be right there." Davies slammed down the phone and stood up.

"Was that about Stuart Wiggins?" Lexy wondered if they'd found the fiancé and hoped that he'd confessed.

"Yes it was." Davies came around the side of the desk and sat on the corner facing Lexy. "He's dead."

Lexy sucked in a breath. She wasn't expecting *that*, but it made perfect sense. He was probably so distraught over killing Veronica that he killed himself. Such a sad thing.

"Did he leave a suicide note? Did he admit to killing Veronica?" Guilt battled with hope in Lexy's chest as she asked the question, feeling bad that someone's suicide could clear her of suspicion.

"Suicide note?" Davies wrinkled her face at Lexy. "Stuart Wiggins didn't commit suicide ... he was murdered."

Chapter Eleven

Lexy drove out of the police station parking lot and pointed her car toward Nans'—she'd called her grandmother with the news of Wiggins' murder as soon as she left the police station and was told to come right over. The news of Wiggins' murder blew their theory all to hell and she needed to brainstorm with Nans and the ladies to try to figure out just what was really going on.

Davies had given her the evil eye before rushing off to the scene of the crime—Lexy had a feeling the detective was seeing Lexy as the killer of all three victims. Of course, it probably didn't help that she had fought with Veronica, discovered the bodies and then was seen at Wiggins' townhouse just yesterday.

She whipped into the *Brooke Ridge Falls Retirement Center* parking lot and sprinted into the building, waited impatiently for Nans to buzz her in, then practically ran to her apartment. The ladies were seated around Nans' dining room table with cups of tea steaming in front of them.

Lexy collapsed into an empty chair, and Nans pushed a mug already filled with hot water toward her.

"Did you tell them about Wiggins?" Lexy asked Nans.

Nans nodded. "There's more to this than a simple murder done in a fit of anger."

"Yeah, but what?" Lexy picked through the basket of herbal teas in the center of Nans' table. Settling on "Lemon Zinger", she dunked the tea bag into the mug, the soothing scent of lemon wafted up to tickle her nose.

"I think we've made some assumptions in this case and it might be best if we start from the beginning ... think it through logically," Ruth said.

"I agree," Helen added.

"Just like we would with any new case." Ida slurped her tea. "Did you bring any pastries?"

Lexy grimaced. "No. Sorry. I rushed over from the police station."

"That's fine, dear." Nans patted her hand. "I have some left over from the other day."

"Helen, help me get out the white board so we can start tracking what we know," Ruth said. The two women got up and headed down the hallway toward Nans' bedrooms while Nans rummaged in the fridge.

A minute later, Helen and Ruth appeared in the hall ... well mostly Helen's backend appeared as she backed down the hall pulling the gigantic whiteboard which stood five feet tall and was about six feet wide. It was set in a wooden frame on wheels so Nans could move it around her apartment easily.

When the ladies were on a case, Nans set up her living and dining area as a command post and the white board stayed out there. If she was having visitors, she could simply wheel it into the spare bedroom.

Nans slid a crystal plate filled with pastries onto the dining room table and Ida eyed them uncertainly. "No biscotti?"

Nans raised a brow. "Really Ida, you can't find something you like on there?"

Ida smiled sheepishly. "Sorry, you know how I love Lexy's biscotti."

"Ahem ..." Ruth stood at the white board, marker in hand. "Are you guys ready to start?"

"Let's list the suspects," Nans said.

The room was silent while everyone thought about the suspects. The only suspect Lexy had was the fiancé, Stuart Wiggins. "Wiggins could have killed Veronica and Philippe, but then who killed Wiggins?"

"Good question," Ida said. "Do you think we have two killers?"

"Perhaps. But I think it's all related to one motive," Nans answered.

"And what's the motive?" Ruth asked.

"Well, at first we thought Wiggins killed Veronica in anger and Philippe just got in the way," Lexy said. "But, maybe there is another motive that we haven't considered."

"The only things that ever drive people to kill are love and money." Helen picked a cheese danish out of the box and bit into the edge.

"What if Philippe was the target and Veronica just got in the way?" Ida asked.

"Then how does Wiggins tie in?" Nans peered at Ida over the dainty china teacup she held to her lips.

"Good question," Ida answered.

"I guess we need to do this the old fashioned way ... list out all the people we need to talk to and then check them off one by one," Helen said.

"Right." Nans tapped her index finger on her lips. "Who do you think could give us information on the *Chez Philippe* murders? Our main suspect for that is Stuart Wiggins but since he's dead we need to talk to anyone he was close to."

Ruth made a "Suspects" column and wrote "Stuart's associates" underneath. She turned to face them. "Can you think of anyone else?"

"If Philippe was the target, then someone close to him might have been the killer—his spouse or significant other," Lexy said.

"Was he married?" Helen asked, taking another dainty bite of the Danish. "I thought he was gay."

"Let's get on the computer and see if we can find out anything about his marital status ... girlfriends —or boyfriends," Nans said. "And while you are at it, let's check his financials ... and Veronica's too."

Ruth made another column with "To Do" at the top and listed the items below it. "How about the fiancé?"

Nans nodded. "Yes, we should check his background and financials too."

"I guess we should also talk to Veronica's friends." Nans turned to Lexy. "Do you know who she was friendly with ... her maid of honor or bridesmaids?"

Lexy grimaced. The *last* person she wanted to talk to was Ramona. "Unfortunately, I do."

"What's her name?" Ruth asked from the whiteboard where she had her pen poised over the surface.

"Ramona Kazlowski."

"Are you friendly with her?" Nans asked. "Can you ask her to lunch or something?"

"Not at all," Lexy said. "She'd probably run the other way if she saw me coming ... especially after the fight at *Chez Philippe*.

"Well, surely she'd be receptive to you if you wanted to give her your condolences on her friend's death," Ida said.

"Doubtful."

"Who else should we talk to?" Nans asked.

"Philippe's staff," Helen answered, and Ruth wrote it down.

"Anyone else?" Ruth asked.

"That's all I can think of," Lexy said. The ladies murmured their agreement.

"So the question is ... just how do we get access to these people?" Ida asked.

"Philippe's staff should be easy. I'm sure the police have their names and addresses on record." Nans slid her eyes toward Lexy. "And we all know Lexy has a way of getting information out of a certain police detective."

Lexy fought the heat creeping into her cheeks.

"And maybe you can find out if all three were shot with the same gun and what type of gun it was while you are at it," Ida added while Ruth scribbled it all down under the "To Do" column.

"I don't know anything about the fiancé," Lexy said. "But Nans said he worked at the Telbourne Museum ... maybe we could ask around there? He might have been close to someone he worked with."

"Good idea," Ruth said, writing it on the board.

Nans walked over to the white board and studied it for a few seconds.

"I think we have a good start," she said, turning to face them. "Once we talk to these people, other clues may be revealed."

"I'll start doing the internet research and looking at the financials," Helen said.

"In the meantime, the rest of us can start asking the questions." Nans looked around the group, her eyes shining with excitement. "You know, I've been dying to go visit that new exhibit at the Telbourne Museum ... who wants to come with me?"

Chapter Twelve

Lexy flipped her phone open and pressed Cassie's number as she pulled out of Nans' parking lot.

"Hey, how did it go at the police station? Did you get your shoe?" Cassie asked.

Lexy's stomach sank. Davies had rushed out to the scene of Wiggins' death and she never did get her shoe. Not that Davies was going to give it to her ... in fact, it seemed like Davies suspected her even more now.

"No. Turns out Veronica's fiancé was murdered too," Lexy said. "So I guess I'm not off the suspect list yet."

"What? Jeez this case sure is turning strange."

"Yeah, tell me about it." Lexy turned left onto her street. "I just came from Nans' and we have a plan in place to question some of the fiancé's coworkers at the museum tomorrow. Can you take over at the bakery?"

"Of course." Cassie's voice crackled over the phone. "Why don't you take the next couple of days off? I'm sure you have lots to do with the wedding plans too. To tell you the truth, I want you out of the kitchen so I can experiment with your cake."

Lexy's heart warmed—she was lucky to have a good friend like Cassie she could trust with her business.

"Thanks Cass," she said. "Why don't you ask Haley if she wants to work some extra hours to help out?" Earlier in the year, Lexy had hired a high school student, Haley, to work in the front after school. It would cost Lexy a little extra but it was nearly impossible to bake in the back room and sell pastries to the customers out front at the same time. Lexy figured Cassie would need the extra help.

"Sounds good—good luck with your interrogations," Cassie said.

Lexy thanked her and hung up the phone just as she pulled up in front of her house. She eyed her parents RV as she got out of the car—she could hear them inside, but wasn't sure she was in the mood for her mother's boundless energy. What she really wanted was to talk to Jack about the case ... and maybe even engage in some activities she *was* in the mood for.

She tiptoed past the RV and was half way to her front door when she heard the door rip open behind her.

"Lexy! I'm so glad you're home!" Vera bounced in the doorway of the RV, her purple and yellow caftan floating up and down like a parachute.

"Hi, Mom."

"I made you're favorite meal ... meatloaf," Vera announced proudly.

Meatloaf *would* taste good right now, Lexy thought. And she didn't have the heart to disappoint her mother.

"That sounds great, Mom."

"Woof!" Sprinkles bounded past Vera's legs aiming straight for Lexy who bent down to scoop the dog up in her arms.

"Hi Sprinks!" Lexy kissed the top of Sprinkles head and the dog wiggled with joy while trying to cover Lexy's face with kisses.

"I brought her over to the RV this morning," Vera said. "I hope you don't mind, but I figured, why should she sit in there all alone when we're right here?"

Lexy gently put Sprinkles on the ground. "No I don't mind at all. I'm glad you did."

"Okay, well dinner will be ready in fifteen minutes, is that okay?"

"Yep, I'll just run in and change, then come right over. Should I bring anything?"

"No. I have everything—even your favorite wine," Vera said as she disappeared back into the RV.

Lexy ran into the house with Sprinkles following happily behind her. She went into the kitchen and poured some dog food in Sprinkles bowl, then snuck a peak out the window at Jack's house.

Was he home?

She craned her neck to see his driveway—his truck was there. Maybe she would eat a quick dinner, and then pretend like she wanted to go to bed early and sneak over to Jack's. She dug in her purse for her cell phone and texted her intentions to Jack, and then ran upstairs to change.

***

The meatloaf was excellent. Afterwards, Lexy endured a battery of measurements her mother said were necessary in order for her to repair the dress which she promised would be done in two days. It was almost two hours later by the time Lexy was able to make her escape.

She raced upstairs and changed into a silky bronze colored top—Jack's favorite. She paired it with white slacks and clear rhinestone studded sandals then took a few minutes to swipe on some makeup and fluff her shoulder length brown hair. Racing through the kitchen, she stopped long enough to grab a bottle of wine and slipped out the back door.

In the backyard, she stopped short. The yard had been decorated with dozens of planters filled with colorful flowers. When did this happen? She narrowed her eyes at her parent's RV. Apparently, her mother had been hard at work.

She shrugged and crossed the backyard, careful to avoid slipping on patches of fallen leaves. She squeezed through the crack in the fence that marked the boundary between her yard and Jack's, and made her way to his back door.

Her heartbeat skittered with excitement as she raised her fist to knock. With all the wedding planning, parents' arrival, and murders, it had been a while since she and Jack had had any alone time and she was looking forward to relaxing with him. Hopefully he would have some news on the case.

Her lips curled in a smile as the door cracked open. Then she heard a woman's laughter drift out from inside and her smile reversed into a frown.

Jack had a woman in there?

Jack appeared at the door and Lexy stared at him confused.

"Lexy, come on in. I thought you didn't feel good." Jack scrunched his brow at her.

He pushed the door wider and she cautiously looked to see who the bimbo laughing in his kitchen was. Her eyes grew wide when she saw who it was ... her mother.

"Lexy, I thought you were going to bed early?" Vera leaned back in her chair to talk to Lexy who was still standing partially behind the door.

Lexy's eyes flitted from her mother to Jack. "You asked my parents here?"

Jack nodded. "Sure, I saw them in the backyard and invited them over for a drink." He frowned when he saw the look on her face and lowered his voice. "Is something wrong?"

"Didn't you get my text?" she whispered.

"No, sorry I had my phone off. Was it important?"

"Nah, never mind." Lexy sighed and then pushed the door open, walked to Jack's cabinet, took out a large wine glass and filled it. Joining her parents at the kitchen table, she let out a sigh—so much for a wild night alone with Jack.

Chapter Thirteen

Lexy, Nans and Ida stood on the steps of the museum looking at the giant concrete building that took up almost a whole city block.

"It sure is big," Ida said.

"Where do we start?" Lexy asked.

"I have a pretty good idea," Nans replied. "Follow me."

She started up the steps. Lexy and Ida fell in beside her. Nans looked at Lexy "Did you get any new clues out of Jack last night?"

"Only that Wiggins was shot with a .22 caliber. The same type of gun that killed Veronica and Philippe."

Nans nodded and reached out to open the glass door that led into the front lobby of the museum. "Ruth discovered that Wiggins made a lot of expensive purchases recently," she whispered as the three of them filed inside.

Ida pursed her lips together. "Well that makes sense with a wedding coming up, they *are* very expensive."

Lexy nodded thinking about all the recent charges on her credit cards—florist, caterer, wedding dress ... *and* Stuart was getting married in Paris. She could only imagine what *that* would cost.

They stood in the cavernous lobby. The marble floor was so shiny Lexy could almost see her reflection. Carved archways set in marble walls opened to hallways that exited from the lobby. A golden sarcophagus sat on the left behind a roped display. To the right, a smiling woman sat behind a large mahogany desk. In front of them, signs on top of a large doorway directed them to various exhibits.

Nans took off toward the dinosaurs. Lexy and Ida followed her down the hall, their footsteps echoing hollowly. She took a right into the dinosaur exhibit that opened up into a giant room. Lexy looked up—the ceiling must have been six stories high. Different types of dinosaurs—Lexy assumed they were life-size since they were so large—loomed around the room. Some just bones, others made to look exactly like they would have when they roamed the earth.

In one corner, a teacher pointed out various aspects of a triceratops to her class of young children. Nans stopped at the Tyrannosaurus Rex display.

"The T-Rex is my favorite," Ida said tilting her head back to look up at the dinosaur.

"I always liked the Velociraptors," Nans replied as she moved to the next exhibit. They made their way slowly around the room. Lexy feigned interest while Nans pointed out different aspects of each exhibit. Lexy was almost ready to fall asleep when their path took them to the security guard who stood next to one of the displays.

"Hello." Nans smiled at the guard.

"Ma'am." The guard nodded.

"It must be wonderful to work in such an interesting place." Nans waved her hand to indicate all the displays. Lexy eyed her cautiously, wondering what she was up to.

"It's a great job," the guard replied patiently.

"Did you know the guard that was killed recently—Stuart Wiggins?" Nans asked. "My granddaughter here was good friends with his fiancée ... such a shame."

Lexy's stomach twisted. *Good friends?*

"It was a shame. I didn't know him well but Eddie Sharp and him were best buds. Eddie usually works the displays in the west wing." The guard pointed to a door on the left in between a skeleton of a bird-like dinosaur and a diorama of a Paleolithic forest floor, complete with dinosaur family and giant ferns.

"Thanks." Nans nodded at the guard. "I'm sure Lexy will want to give her condolences, right Lexy?"

"Umm ... yeah, right. Of course," Lexy stammered. She wasn't nearly as comfortable lying as Nans.

Nans took off toward the door and Lexy practically had to sprint to keep up with her. They marched into the next room and Lexy felt her breath catch in her throat—it was like going into a different world. Glass cases loaded with sparkly jewelry and gems lined all four sides of the room. In the center, tall glass displays filled with crowns were lined up in a row. Each display had its own lighting, which seemed to be calibrated to coax the maximum amount of sparkle out of each and every facet of each and every gemstone.

Ida summed up Lexy's thoughts in one word. "Wow."

Nans wasn't distracted by the glitter—she had a job to do. She marched right over to the guard standing in the corner.

"Are you Eddie?" Nans asked

The guard's eyes flickered from Nans, to Lexy, to Ida, uncertainly. "Yes."

"We heard we could find you here. We wanted to tell you how sorry we are about Stuart and Veronica." Nans gestured to Lexy. "Lexy here went to school with Veronica and she's quite broken up about the whole thing."

Lexy nodded and tried to act "broken up."

"Really?" Eddie frowned at Lexy. "I don't think we've ever met."

"Oh, sorry." Lexy stuck her hand out. "Lexy Baker. Veronica and I recently reconnected so I didn't know a lot of her friends yet." Lexy soothed her conscious by telling herself it wasn't really a lie. She and Veronica *had* recently reconnected ... just not in the friendly way she was implying.

Eddie shook her hand, his eyes darting around the room nervously. Lexy wondered if it was against the rules to shake hands with the customers.

"It's just such a mystery," Nans said. "Do you have any idea what they were into that would have made someone want to kill them?"

Eddie's eyes went wide, he shuffled his feet. "I don't know what you mean."

Nans leaned in closer to him and whispered. "Well, they *were* murdered. Must have been a reason."

Lexy watched Eddie's face harden as he narrowed his eyes at Nans. "Veronica *was* acting kind of odd—I figured that was due to the upcoming wedding. But her friend Ramona was acting really strange, too."

Nan's perked up. "Oh? In what way?"

"I don't know. Jittery. Like something was going on."

"Any idea what they were up to?"

Eddie shrugged, then glanced around the room again. "Sorry lady I shouldn't be talking so much."

He stepped backwards away from Nans, bumped into one of the displays and whirled around, relaxing when he saw what he had bumped into.

Nans' eyebrows rose up. Lexy knew what she was thinking—Eddie sure was nervous.

"Well, thanks for your time and we're sorry for your loss," Nans said and then turned and walked toward the exit.

***

On the way out of the museum, Nans' cell phone erupted into a chorus of bird tweets. She stopped and opened her giant old-lady purse handing Lexy a flashlight, small packet of tissues, container of Tums, a tube of lipstick and a mirror before she found the phone.

While Nans fiddled with her phone, Lexy returned the items to the purse.

"It's your parents ... they want to meet me for lunch." Nans sounded disappointed. "I'd really like to continue on this investigation, but I hate to put them off since they'll only be here a short time."

"We could meet for a quick lunch, maybe?" Lexy suggested.

"Is that okay with you, Ida?"

"Sure, why not? I love a free lunch," Ida said.

Nans slid her eyes over to Ida as she punched the buttons on her phone. "I didn't say anything about *free*."

Ida shrugged and laughed. "It never hurts to ask."

"Hi Roy," Nans chirped into the phone. "It would be lovely to meet you for lunch. I'm actually out with Lexy now ... she took Ida and me to the senior center. Maybe the three of us could meet at *The Streetcar Diner* ... say in forty-five minutes?"

Lexy lifted a brow at Nans. She had to admit she was becoming mildly concerned with the ease her grandmother could spit out lies.

"Okay. Great. See you then." Nans snapped the phone shut.

"Senior Center?" Lexy asked.

Nans laughed. "Well I couldn't very well tell them what we're up to. Believe me, the less Roy and Vera know about my sleuthing, the better for all of us. And I'm sure you don't want them knowing that *you're* a suspect in a triple murder."

"True," Lexy said. "I guess a little white lie never hurt anyone."

They hopped into Lexy's VW Beetle and headed back to Brooke Ridge Falls. Almost forty minutes later, they pulled into the parking lot at *The Streetcar Diner*. The old fashioned diner sat smack in the middle of the downtown area and was decorated to look like a streetcar on the outside and an old fashioned diner on the inside. Lexy parked in the side lot. Her parents RV was already there taking up a good portion of the small lot. Lexy wondered how her father had maneuvered it in there without hitting something.

Bells tinkled as Lexy pulled open the door and stood back to let Nans and Ida enter ahead of her. She searched the gleaming interior of the diner for her parents, her eyes flitting over the glass pedestal cake displays standing on the steel edged Formica counter. A row of round stools sat in front of the counter, their red Naugahyde tops twirling on gleaming steel bases. Behind the counter, Lexy could see through to the kitchen, which was abuzz with activity.

"Yoo-hoo! Over here!" Lexy heard her mother's voice over the din of conversation and clanking plates. Turning toward the voice, she saw her mother waving frantically from a booth next to the window. Even without the frantic waving, it would have been hard not to notice Vera with the brilliant red shirt plastered with appliqué leaves in orange and yellow she was wearing. Lexy glanced at her father in a plain white shirt, feeling relief for him that her mother hadn't forced him to wear a shirt that matched hers.

They slid into the booth, Lexy next to her father and Nans and Ida beside her mother. Greetings were exchanged and then everyone buried their faces in the glossy plastic covered menus.

"What are you getting?" Lexy asked her father.

"The chicken club." He closed his menu and returned it to the metal holder at the edge of the table.

"I'm trying to watch what I eat, so I'm just getting pie and a coffee," Vera announced.

"Pie sounds good to me," Ida said sliding her menu into the holder.

"The heck with you light eaters. I'm getting a cheeseburger, fries and a chocolate milkshake." Nans slapped her menu shut.

"I think a grilled cheese will hit the spot for me." Lexy always craved a good grilled cheese once the weather started to turn and, even though it was still early fall with warm days, the nights were getting colder.

"So, how was the senior center?" Vera asked.

Lexy looked at Nans who didn't skip a beat. "Oh, it was lovely. They were giving out flu shots so Ida and I wanted to take advantage of that. Plus we got to see Merna Fisk's crochet toilet paper covers."

Lexy bit the side of her cheek and looked out the window to keep from laughing. The diner was across the street from *Chez Philippe* and it looked like someone was inside.

Shouldn't the shop be closed for the investigation?

She squinted and leaned closer to the window. A movement inside caught her eye. Someone *was* in there!

The waitress came and she tore herself away from the window to order. She kicked Nans under the table and jerked her head at the window to get Nans attention.

Nans jumped. "Is something wrong dear?"

Everyone at the table stared at Lexy. She didn't want to say anything in front of her parents. If her mother got wind of the investigation, there's no telling what she would do.

Lexy's mouth said "No." But she stared at Nans, her eyes saying yes. Apparently, Nans didn't get it though, because she merely gave Lexy a funny look then continued on with the conversation the rest of them were having.

"… notions for your wedding dress." Vera's voice penetrated Lexy's thoughts.

"What?" Lexy asked. *Notions?* Weren't notions sewing things … like the leaves Vera had appliquéd to the garish shirt she wore? Lexy had a sudden image of her beautiful sophisticated gown cluttered up with oversized pieces of lace, buttons and colorful leaf appliqués.

"I don't think my dress needs any *notions,*" Lexy said. "I had it custom designed, you know. I want it exactly the way it is."

"Custom designed?" Vera frowned at Lexy. "I hope it wasn't that Philippe guy … I heard about the messy business at his shop."

Lexy's stomach pinched. "Oh? What did you hear?"

Vera leaned forward and lowered her voice. "He was murdered … along with some young girl. Maybe his lover … he was almost seventy but still looked quite good for his age. Anyway, I heard he had gotten into financial trouble so that probably had something to do with the murder."

Lexy exchanged a look with Ida and Nans. "Where did you hear about the financial trouble?"

"Oh, you know—around town." Vera waved her hand in the air. "Anyway, I'm not changing anything on your dress … I just need some pieces so I can let it out a bit. According to my measurements, it's a little small for you. Did you gain weight since you had it fitted?"

Lexy bristled at the comment, then remembered how the bust *had* seemed a little tight when she last tried it on in the shop. She didn't think she'd gained weight but she'd been so busy with wedding plans she hadn't exactly been paying attention to the scales.

"Oh, here comes our food," Vera announced saving Lexy from having to think any more about her weight gain.

The waitress set the plates in front of them and all conversation stopped while everyone focused on their lunch. Lexy leaned against the cushioned Naugahyde backrest and contemplated her grilled cheese. Cheese was fattening, wasn't it? Maybe she should have ordered a salad. Her stomach grumbled in disagreement. She picked up the sandwich and nibbled on an edge.

Her attention drifted across the street to *Chez Philippe*. Someone was definitely in there ... going from the front room to the back. She needed to get over there right away, but how could she brush off her parents without hurting their feelings?

"Are you going to eat all those fries?" she asked Nans while covertly jerking her head toward the window.

"Help yourself." Nans turned her plate so the side with the fries was facing Lexy. "Is something wrong with your neck?"

Lexy widened her eyes and looked toward the window. "No."

Nans squinted at her, then her face dawned with understanding and she looked out the window, her eyes lighting up when she realized where Lexy was looking.

Nans shoved the last of her burger into her mouth then reached for the stainless steel napkin holder on the end of the table. Pulling out several small square napkins, she used them to wrap the rest of her fries and shoved the package into her purse.

"Well, we'd better hurry," Nans said.

Ida looked up from her pie. "What? I'm still working on the whipped topping here."

"We don't want to miss your orthopedic shoe appointment," Lexy said feeling a little dismayed at how easy she came up with the lie—almost as easy as Nans. Maybe lying ran in the family.

Ida scrunched up her face. "But I don—"

Lexy kicked her under the table and gave her 'the look'. Ida's eyes went wide and she continued.

"—t want to miss that appointment. No siree. I missed it last week and there was hell to pay." Ida shoved the rest of the pie in her mouth and blotted her lips with a napkin.

Lexy's father pushed his empty plate away. "I'm ready to go myself. What about you Vera?"

"Oh sure," Vera twittered as she sipped the last of her coffee. As if on cue, the waitress brought the check. Lexy's dad insisted on paying.

"You guys go so that you can get to your appointment."

"Thanks, Dad." Lexy gave him a peck on the cheek before sliding out of the booth. She blew her mom a kiss while she herded Nans and Ida toward the door.

"There's someone in *Chez Philippe*!" Lexy said as soon as they were outside. Nans and Ida looked over at the store just in time to see a shadow move in the corner.

"I see it! Let's go confront them—we have the element of surprise on our side!" Ida started across the street and Nans grabbed her arm to pull her back.

"Not yet," Nans said. "We have to move Lexy's car, otherwise Vera and Roy might recognize it in the parking lot when they leave."

They hustled over to Lexy's car and drove around the block until they saw the RV drive away. Lexy pulled into a spot in front of *Chez Philippe* and they tumbled out of the car and sprinted to the door.

Lexy stopped short, her hand on the cold metal door handle. "This could be dangerous."

"Great! We love danger, right Ida?" Nans looked at Ida who nodded.

Lexy took a deep breath and tried the door. It was open. She slipped inside with Nans and Ida right behind her.

Light filtered into the main room from the back and Lexy could hear muffled noises. Someone was back there.

"Should we announce ourselves, or surprise them?" Ida whispered.

"We don't want to tip them off. Let's keep quiet and maybe we'll catch them in the act." Nans tiptoed toward the back room. Lexy's stomach tightened as she followed her. That could be the killer back there—maybe this wasn't such a good idea.

Nans stood against the wall next to the opening to the back room. She poked her head around the doorway, then motioned Lexy and Ida to follow her in. Lexy stood in the doorway, confused. Standing with her back to them and holding one of the drawers from her sewing cabinet was Philippe's seamstress.

"Millie?" Lexy asked.

Millie whirled around. The box fell from her hands clattering on the floor, beads and pearls bounced all over the place. She had her silver hair up in a bun; some strands had loosened and framed her heart-shaped face. For the first time Lexy realized that Millie was still quite attractive for a woman nearing seventy.

Millie's hands flew up to her heart. "What are *you* doing here?"

Lexy immediately felt bad for frightening the woman. "I'm so sorry. I didn't mean to startle you." She ran over to the fallen box and started herding the beads back into it.

"We saw someone in here and came to investigate," Nans explained. "Isn't the shop closed due to the ... umm ... events of the past week?"

"The police are done with their investigation," Millie said briskly. "I came in to finish up some of the dresses. Even though the shop is technically closed, the brides still need their gowns."

"It's such a shame ... what happened," Ida said.

"So senseless, I mean why would someone kill that nice man?" Nans question sounded innocent enough, but Lexy knew it was designed to get Millie to talk about any suspicions she had. Lexy was finding the job of rounding up all the errant beads impossible so she shoved as many of them as she could into the box and stood up, holding the box out to Millie.

"I have no idea," Millie said snatching the box from Lexy.

"Well, if something was amiss in the business ... or Mr. Montague's personal life, I'm sure you would have noticed." Nans winked at her. "The assistants always know everything."

Millie put down the box and grabbed scissors and a roll of lace with trembling hands.

"There was nothing amiss here," she said sharply, her eyes darted around the room to avoid looking directly at Nans. "Now if you ladies don't mind. I need to get to work on these dresses."

"Of course. Sorry to bother you," Nans said and turned to leave.

Lexy and Ida muttered good-byes and followed Nans out to Lexy's car. As they buckled themselves in, Nans said, "Well, I'd say our day today was very productive. Let's go back to my place and fill everything in on the board."

"Yeah," Ida said. "And we might move Millie to our suspect list."

Lexy's brow creased. "Why is that?"

"Did you see the way her hands were shaking?" Ida asked. "I can guarantee she must have been very nervous about something."

"How do you know?"

"She can't be that shaky normally—no seamstress could sew worth a darn with quivering hands like that."

Chapter Fourteen

Lexy settled into the recliner in Nans' living room savoring the bitter taste of the strong coffee in the mug she held in her hand. She needed the caffeine to get her through the rest of the day—keeping up with Nans was exhausting.

"So, did you uncover any new clues?" Helen stood next to the white board, which was directly in front of Lexy.

"Yes. And we knocked off some items from our 'to do' list," Ida answered from a chair on the other side of the room.

"You tell us what you found first, and then I'll tell you what I found." Ruth pulled a dining room chair over next to Lexy, setting her iPad and a cup of tea on the side table.

"Well, we went to the museum first thing. They have some great displays there, we really should go some time," Nans said.

"That's nice." Helen shot Nans a sarcastic look. "But did you find anything relevant to the case?"

"I'm getting to that." Nans walked over to the white board and pointed at one of the lines. "We talked to Stuart Wiggins' friend at the museum ... Eddie something his name was. He seemed unusually nervous, didn't he Lexy?"

"Yes. And he said Veronica and Ramona were acting strange."

Helen's brows shot up. "Oh really? Do you think they were up to something?"

"Hard to say," Nans said. "But let's write that down on the board."

Helen turned and scribbled on the board. "Should we put this Eddie under suspects? What about Veronica and Ramona?"

Nans pressed her lips together. "I think so ... we might as well list everyone who acts strange and then we'll work on weeding through the list to see who had motive and opportunity."

"Of course, we still don't know what the motive is," Ida mumbled around a mouthful of cream cheese brownie.

"I might have a line on that," Ruth said. Everyone turned to look at her. "I was able to get into Philippe's bank account and it seems he had a very large deposit a few months ago."

"How large?" Nans asked.

"Fifty thousand dollars."

Ida whistled. "That sounds like a lot ... but with a business like his, maybe that's not so unusual."

"That's the thing," Ruth said. "It wasn't in his business account. It was in his personal account.

He normally didn't have deposits anywhere near that high."

Lexy chewed her bottom lip. "I wonder if that has anything to do with what my mom said about his business being in trouble or the break in at *Chez Philippe*?"

"Yeah, maybe he needed money to save his business, so he did something underhanded that paid good and someone broke in to steal the money," Ida said.

"Yeah ... but what would he have done for fifty thou?" Nans asked.

Ida shrugged. "Who knows? I saw an episode of *Castle* where the guy got laid off from his job and needed money so he ended up being a drug mule."

"Well I highly doubt Philippe would do that. And even if he *was* up to something, how do Stuart, Victoria, Ramona and Eddie play into it?" Ruth asked.

"And don't forget Millie," Ida added.

"Millie?" Helen's brows creased.

Ida nodded. "At lunch today we saw someone skulking around inside *Chez Philippe*. So we went in to apprehend the perp. It was this Millie lady ... his seamstress I guess, right Lexy?"

"Yep." Lexy sipped her coffee. "She said the police told her she could go in and finish the gowns they had on order. She *did* seem rather nervous ... and not at all friendly."

Ruth tapped the marker on the whiteboard. "If Philippe was into something shady, it makes sense that Millie might know about it."

"She's been his seamstress for a long time so she might be protective of him, too," Lexy added.

"Or in on it with him," Ida said.

"It doesn't make sense that Veronica and Stuart would have anything to do with it, though," Ruth said.

Lexy sighed. "Right. This is all so confusing."

"Well at least we have more of a clue about the motive. If we could just figure out where that money came from." Nans turned to Ruth. "Can you dig around to find the source?"

Ruth nodded. "I can try."

"And we also need to talk to this Ramona. She's the only one on the list we haven't talked to."

Lexy cringed. "I don't know how we're going to do that ... she hates me."

Ida snapped her fingers. "I know!"

"You do?" Lexy asked.

"She was Veronica's best friend, right?"

Lexy nodded.

"Well then it makes sense she would be at the wake," Ida said with a gleam in her eye.

‘That’s right!” Nans said. “We need to find out when the wake is and attend it. You know what we always say ...”

Lexy, Ida, Ruth and Helen chorused the answer. “The best place to find out about the murder is at the victim’s wake!”

***

Lexy coasted to a stop in front of her house. Quietly closing her car door, she tiptoed past the RV. She wasn’t avoiding her parents—she just needed some quiet time to think about the day’s events and tend to some of the wedding tasks she’d been putting off in favor of investigating the murders. She still had a lot to get done, like picking out the flowers for her bouquet, choosing the appetizers for the reception and deciding which music to use for the ceremony.

Was her wedding really in a few days? She pushed away the panic that clutched at her chest as she slid her key into the lock on the front door. Her heart stopped when the door swung wide open before the key even made it all the way in.

She stood frozen in the doorway, her stomach sinking ... her house had been ransacked!

Drawers had been flung open. Everything had been ripped from the closet and thrown on the floor. Even the cushions had been torn from the couch. Tears welled up in her eyes, and then fear seized her.

Where was Sprinkles?

"Sprinkles!" She ran into the house praying the little white dog would come bounding out from one of the rooms. She barely noticed the kitchen was in a shambles as she ran upstairs stopping short at the door to her bedroom, which was a mess of piled up clothes. Her dresser drawers had been thrown on the floor and everything removed from her closet.

What the heck were they looking for? And what had they done with Sprinkles?

Lexy remembered her mother had taken Sprinkles to the RV the day before. Maybe she was in there now. She ran back down the stairs praying that whoever had done this hadn't also gotten into the RV and done something even worse to her parents.

She bolted out into the yard and over to the RV. Ripping open the door, she sprinted into the RV, much to the surprise of her mother who stood in the kitchen cutting up a tomato.

"Lexy, what in the world are you doing?"

Sprinkles jumped off the couch yapping happily and Lexy burst into tears as she bent down, scooped up the dog and covered her with kisses.

"What's the matter?" Her father's concern made her cry even more.

"Someone broke into my house!" She sputtered.

Vera gasped. "What? Are you okay?"

Lexy nodded, accepting the tissue her father handed her.

"Did they take anything?" Roy asked.

"I don't know. I didn't look around very good. I was worried about Sprinkles and you guys." Lexy blew her nose on the tissue. "Did you see anyone here today?"

Vera and Roy looked at each other. "No. But we were gone most of the day in the RV."

Lexy whipped out her cell phone. "I have to call Jack."

Vera rubbed Lexy's back and made soothing noises as she put in the call. Jack was at work, but said he'd drop everything and rush over.

"Don't go back in the house," he warned.

Lexy waited for him on the steps of the RV with her mom and dad. As soon as he stepped out of the car, Lexy flew into his arms, tears pricking her eyes. Jack made the appropriate hugging and patting motions and Lexy disentangled herself after a few seconds, feeling a little embarrassed.

She was usually much stronger than this. She barely even flinched, now, when she stumbled across a dead body. But for some reason, this break in at her house really bothered her. *This* was personal.

Jack held both her hands, his liquid brown eyes full of concern. “Are you okay to go back in there?”

“Yeah, I’m okay ... now that you’re here.”

Jack led her inside with her parents and Sprinkles following close behind. “Wow, they really did mess the place up.”

“You can say that again,” Vera said from behind Lexy.

The four of them stood there surveying the damage while Sprinkles ran around sniffing everything.

“Too bad Sprinkles can’t talk. She probably knows exactly who did this,” Roy said.

“And what they were after,” Jack added then turned to Lexy. “Is anything missing?”

“I don’t know. It’s hard to tell with all this mess.” She didn’t really have anything valuable, just a few antique vases that Nans had given her, but they were in their usual place on the mantle. It looked like everything was still there, just messed up.

“I don’t think anything is missing,” she said.

Jack was still holding her hand and he tugged her forward. "Let's go room by room and you can tell me if you notice anything before Davies comes."

"Lexy's heart lurched. "Davies?"

"Sorry sweetie. I had to tell her. This could be related to the murders." Jack pushed a lock of hair behind Lexy's ear. "Besides, she's not so bad once you get to know her."

Lexy made a face. She doubted that.

"Murders?" Vera asked.

Lexy cringed. The cat was out of the bag.

"You remember, Mom, the dress designer Philippe? He was designing my dress." Lexy waved her hand dismissively as if it was nothing to worry about.

"Why would that have something to do with this?" Vera frowned at the messy room.

"Oh, it doesn't, but the detective in charge is a little ... umm ... overzealous. And since he was designing my dress ..." Lexy let her voice trail, off hoping the lame excuse satisfied her mother's curiosity.

As if on cue, a car screeched to a stop in front of the house. Turning to look through the large living room window, she saw Davies jump out of a dark sedan with flashing blue and red lights on top.

"Great," Lexy muttered. "Now the whole neighborhood will know."

Davies appeared in the doorway wearing her all black outfit again, but this time with mid-calf black boots adorned with lots of buckles.

"What happened in here?" She stood with her feet shoulder width apart, fists on her hips.

"Someone broke in and tossed the place," Jack said.

"I can see *that* ... but why?" Davies demanded.

"How would I know?" Lexy asked.

"Maybe you did it yourself to throw suspicion away from you." Davies eyes scanned the room.

"Hey, now wait a minute." Jack stepped toward Davies. "Lexy wouldn't do something like that. And besides, she's not guilty of anything."

Davies held her hand up. "Just covering all the angles." She crossed to the kitchen and looked in. "Is the whole house like this?"

"Yep. Even upstairs," Lexy said.

"Is anything missing?"

"Not that I can tell. I don't really have anything worth stealing except maybe these vases and some china in the china cabinet, but it's all still here."

Davies blew out a small bubble of pink gum, then sucked it back in again.

"Do you have any enemies or know anyone who would want to toss the place?"

Lexy shook her head. "No."

Davies took out her cell phone. "I'm going to take some pictures. You'll have to go through everything thoroughly and let me know if anything is missing. If they didn't break in to steal stuff, then they must have been looking for something. Do you have any idea what that might be."

Lexy's stomach sank. *What would anyone be looking for in her house?* "I have no idea. Do you think this could be related to the murders?"

Davies lowered the camera and stared at Lexy. "I thought you had nothing to do with that other than finding the bodies."

"I didn't," Lexy said. "But maybe whoever killed Philippe was looking for something and they *think* I have it ... or that I know something. Wasn't *Chez Philippe* broken into after the murders? Maybe they got my name from the customer files."

"Customer files?" Davies asked.

"Yeah, I heard the place was searched," Lexy answered.

"It was. But not the customer files. The sewing area. All the little lace ribbons and beads were thrown all over the floor. It was a real mess ... much like this place." Davies spread her arms to indicate the mess on Lexy's floor.

Lexy felt her brow wrinkle. *Why would someone search the sewing area?* She didn't have long to ponder as a sharp knock sounded on her front door, which had been sitting wide open all this time.

Everyone spun around to see her neighbor, Mr. Johnston, standing in the doorway looking at her living room in dismay.

"Hi, Mr. Johnston." Lexy crossed over to the elderly man.

"Lexy what's happened here? Are you all right?" he asked.

"Yes. Everyone is fine." Lexy patted his arm. "Someone broke in."

"Oh, I saw the flashing lights from my house," he gestured toward the house across the street, "and I came over to see if you needed any help."

"Oh no, we're fine," Lexy said.

"Okay then. Let me know if you need anything." He turned to leave.

"Wait a minute," Davies called after him and Johnston turned back around. "You didn't by any chance happen to see anything strange going on here today?"

Mr. Johnston puckered his face. "Well, I don't spend the whole day spying on my neighbors. But I did see the big rig out there pull out in the morning. Of course Lexy was gone to work early in the day and then in the afternoon a red Toyota was here for a while."

"A red Toyota?" Davies perked up. "Did you get the plates?"

Mr. Johnston rubbed his hands nervously. "Plates? Well no, I didn't realize I would have to do that. Do you think that's the person who did this?"

"Possibly," Davies said. "Do you remember how long the car was here?"

"I'm not sure. I was watching my shows when I first saw it and then I had my afternoon tea. Next time I looked it was gone ... so maybe an hour or two."

"Okay. Thanks." Davies pecked away at the keys of her Smartphone. Lexy assumed that was her version of taking notes.

"You don't think it's dangerous around here now, do you?" Mr. Johnson lingered in the doorway.

"No, not at all," Davies said. "This is an isolated case—you have nothing to worry about."

Johnston nodded, looked at Lexy uncertainly, and then shuffled off across the street.

“Well, that’s an odd coincidence,” Lexy said.

“What’s that?” Jack asked as Davies resumed her picture taking.

“Stuart Wiggins’ neighbor told us that Veronica drove a red Toyota Corolla. But she’s dead, so either someone used her car to break in here or that’s one heck of a coincidence.”

Davies scrunched her face up at Lexy. “Who told you that?”

“The fiancé’s neighbor. He saw her peel out in it after they had a fight.”

“Well that’s strange. We towed Veronica’s car from *Chez Philippe* to the station to search it for evidence. We have it there right now, but it’s not a red Toyota ... it’s a black Prius.”

Chapter Fifteen

Lexy spent most of the night cleaning up the mess in her house with the help of Jack, her parents, and a couple bottles of wine, so she slept in the next morning. She hadn’t found anything missing, unless you counted two pairs of red lace panties that she couldn’t seem to find. Oddly enough, she found something extra—a gold cross on a chain that definitely wasn't hers. She set it aside figuring it was probably her mother's.

Nans had left her a message that Veronica's wake was that afternoon, so she scooted over to the florist and chose a gorgeous bouquet of white lilies and roses before heading over to pick the ladies up for the wake.

Despite her misgivings at attending Veronica's wake and seeing Ramona, Lexy couldn't help but smile at the clear blue sky as she drove to the retirement center. The gorgeous crisp fall morning had given way to a warm afternoon, which was the perfect weather for the champagne colored silk sleeveless blouse and black pencil skirt Lexy had chosen from the rumpled pile of clothes on her closet floor.

She pulled up to the front of the retirement center where Nans, Ida, Ruth and Helen were all waiting for her, each dressed in a beige trench coat and holding a gigantic patent leather purse. She jumped out of the car and pushed the front seat forward, marveling at how easily Ruth, Ida and Helen could contort themselves to fit into the back of the small VW Beetle.

"I'm still amazed that you guys can get into this car so easily," Lexy said.

"Oh Pffft ..." Ruth answered. "We take yoga and Pilates. This is easy. Try playing twister with the folks down on the first floor and you'll see what difficult is."

Nans, Ida and Helen laughed at her joke—Lexy had no idea what she was talking about and figured she was probably better off that way, so she didn't ask.

"You guys won't believe what happened last night," Lexy said as she pulled out of the parking lot.

"What?"

"My house got broken into ... they ransacked it."

Nans gasped. "Are you okay?"

"Yep, I'm fine. Sprinkles was in the RV with Mom and Dad and they weren't even there. It must have happened sometime in the afternoon. I discovered it when I got home from your place."

"Was it a robbery?" Helen asked.

"No. Nothing was taken." She didn't feel the need to mention the panties—they were probably at Jack's.

Nans pressed her lips together. "This has to do with the murder case, doesn't it?"

"I think so, but I can't imagine why," Lexy said. "I don't know anything about the murders."

"Maybe someone thinks you are asking too many questions," Ida offered.

"Hmm ... Maybe." Lexy's stomach clenched at the thought. Was the break-in a warning? "I found out a couple of other interesting tidbits about the case."

"Do tell," Nans said.

Lexy pulled into a parking spot in the back corner of the funeral home lot and turned in her seat so she could see the ladies in the back. "You know how *Chez Philippe* was broken into the night after the murders?"

Four gray heads nodded in unison.

"Well, I just assumed they were looking for something in the files," Lexy continued, "information or customer's names. But they weren't."

"What were they looking for?" Ida asked.

"I don't know exactly, but they didn't search the files. They searched the sewing area."

Ruth's brows lifted a fraction of an inch. "What could someone possibly want in there?"

Lexy shrugged. "Who knows? But it's interesting that that's where Millie was when we saw her there yesterday."

"Yeah, that sure is something to think about." Helen rummaged in her purse, then, much to Lexy's surprised, pulled out an iPad. "I'm just going to make a note to look into that further."

"Well, if you guys liked that, *this* is even better." Lexy leaned forward, toward the ladies. "Stuart Wiggins' neighbor told us that Wiggins had a fight with a woman—we assumed it was Veronica—shortly before she was killed. He said he saw her speed off in a red Toyota."

"So?" Ida asked.

"Detective Davies told me that Veronica drove a black Prius."

"Then who was in the red Toyota?" Ruth asked.

"That's what we need to find out," Lexy said as she pushed her door open and climbed out of the car.

Helen stuffed the iPad back into her purse as they walked toward the McGreevey funeral home. The heavy glass and oak doors swung open as if by magic as they approached and two gray-suited gentlemen ushered them in.

The somber energy hit Lexy as soon as she walked inside. The faint sound of hymnal music blended with hushed conversation and the sweet smell of freshly cut flowers dragged at her heart driving home the gravity of the occasion.

The four of them stood in the entryway of the centuries old mansion. In front of them, a tasteful sign gave directions to the different viewings. Apparently, business was good for old Mr.

McGreevey, because there were three viewings today.

"We're in luck!" Ida whispered as she pointed to the sign. Not only was Veronica being waked here, but Philippe was also.

"We can kill two birds with one stone," Nans whispered back. "Ida, Ruth and Helen—you go check out Philippe's wake, Lexy and I will tackle Veronica's. Looks like it's in the *Rose Petal* room.

The ladies were no strangers to wakes, especially at McGreevey's, and Nans knew exactly where the *Rose Petal* room was. Lexy followed her down the hall, stopping only to peak into the small narrow alcove they used for refreshments. She noticed with dismay that they had grocery store cookies out on trays. How tacky. She made a mental note to talk to McGreevy about a discounted price if he wanted to offer cookies and pastry from her bakery.

Nans grabbed her arm and propelled her into the *Rose Petal* room. Lexy's throat constricted as she looked at Veronica laid out in her casket. Even though she hadn't gotten along with Veronica, she certainly didn't wish *this* on her. Glancing around the room, she noticed it was practically empty.

Veronica's parents, sister and brother stood on the other side of the casket. About a dozen people sat in the metal folding chairs that had been setup in rows. Eddie Sharp stood in the corner shooting angry looks at them. Lexy elbowed Nans in the ribs and nodded her head toward the corner.

Nans started toward Eddie, whose eyes widened as he realized they were headed straight for him.

"Aren't you the nice young man from the museum?" Nans asked.

"Yes," Eddie said, his eyes darting to the left and then right. *Probably looking for an escape route*, Lexy thought.

"Oh it must be terrible having your friend and his fiancé to mourn." Nans shook her head and made tsking sounds. "Did you know Veronica well?"

"Not as well as I knew Stu," Eddie answered.

"You and he must have been very close," Nans said. "I mean for you to come here to mourn his fiancé. I bet you probably were the types of friends that did everything together."

Eddie shrugged. "Well, not everything."

"But surely, you must have known them well enough to have some idea about what got them killed," Nans said.

"Listen lady, I don't know anything ... but if you want to know who was close enough to Veronica to know *everything*, then you might ask her." Eddie slid his eyes to the left. Lexy's heart leaped into her throat when she realized who he was looking at.

Ramona.

Ramona looked up and their eyes met, sending a jolt through Lexy. Ramona's eyes widened and she took a step toward them.

"You!"

Lexy fought the urge to run as Ramona advanced on them. Out of the corner of her eye, she could see the other mourners had turned to look at them. She glanced back at Eddie, but the corner was empty—he'd made his escape.

"Just what do you think you are doing here?" Ramona demanded.

Nans drew herself up to her full five-foot-one height and said, "We're paying our respects."

Ramona ignored Nans and stepped close to Lexy, her face so close that Lexy could smell she'd had a liverwurst sandwich for lunch. "Listen, Miss Busybody. You better stick to your own business and get out of Veronica's."

"What *do* you mean?" Lexy feigned ignorance.

"You know damn well what I mean. You've always had it in for Veronica and now you've been meddling around and making things worse for everyone. Can't you leave Veronica alone, especially now when she's dead?" Ramona's voice rose to a shriek as she said the last five words.

Lexy's pulse surged. She could feel everyone in the room staring at her. A dark-suited man hovered in the doorway—probably one of the McGreevy's ready to throw them out if they caused more of a scene. Nans pulled at her elbow to leave, but Lexy jerked her arm free.

"Whoa, wait a minute." Lexy held her palms up in front of her. "The last thing I want to do is make things worse. And I have no idea what you mean by meddling."

"You're a liar just like you were in high school." Ramona spat the words at her.

"I don't understand why you're so upset." Lexy narrowed her eyes at Ramona. "Do you have something to hide?"

Nans tugged on Lexy's arm again as Ramona shot daggers at Lexy with her eyes. The guy in the suit started toward them and Lexy realized Nans had the right idea. They should get out of there before they made more of a scene. Lexy let Nans drag her out of the room into the large hall.

She leaned against the wall and puffed out her cheeks, the blast of air sending her bangs flying.

"Boy, she was madder than a cat in a bathtub," Nans said.

"Yeah, but didn't that seem kind of excessive?" Lexy asked.

"Well, look who's here." Lexy's stomach twisted at the sound of the voice behind her. She spun around, coming face to face with Detective Davies.

"What brings *you* here, Baker?" Davies asked.

"Why, we're just paying our respects." Nans answered for both of them.

"Oh really! Is that all?" Davies chomped her gum as she narrowed her eyes at them.

"Yep," Lexy said. "What brings you here?"

"Oh, didn't you know? Detecting 101—always go to the wake." Davies baby blues lit up with amusement. As she brushed past Lexy on her way into the *Rose Petal* room, she threw one parting comment over her shoulder. "They say you can usually find the killer at the wake ... and look—here *you* are."

***

"Well, I think we may not want to press our luck here," Nans said as she watched Detective Davies disappear into the *Rose Petal* room. "Let's see if the others have anything to report."

They headed toward the *Velvet Slumber* room where Philippe was. Passing the refreshment alcove, they saw Ida, Ruth and Helen bending over a table of cookies. Each of them were piling cookies into large napkins they held in their hands.

"Uhh hmm," Nans said from the doorway.

The three ladies jumped, then whirled around, the cookie laden napkins behind their backs.

"Oh, Mona it's you." Ruth's cheeks were bright pink.

Nans walked into the room, closer to her friends. Lexy wandered over to one of the tables and picked up a shortbread cookie.

"Did you find anything out?" Nans said in a low voice.

Lexy inspected the cookie, it *looked* fine. She bit in, nibbling the edge and turning the small piece of cookie around in her mouth. Too sweet. Not crispy enough.

"There's not much going on in there," Ruth said wrapping her stack of cookies up in the napkin and shoving it in her purse.

"We did see that Millie lady though," Helen added.

"She wasn't very happy to see *me*," Ida said as she shoved her cookie package into her black patent leather purse. "She called me a busybody!"

Nans and the other ladies laughed at Ida's indignation.

"She seemed right mad," Ida said as Lexy tossed the rest of her cookie in the trash. "If you ask me, she could be the killer with the way she's acting."

Helen nodded her head. "It sure seems like she has something to hide."

"What did you guys find out?" Ruth looked from Nans to Lexy.

"Oh, we had a little run-in over there." Nans glanced out in the hall. "Let's get out of here and we'll tell you about it in the car."

The ladies secured their purses and marched down the main hallway, through the foyer and out the front door. Just as they were stepping down from the last granite step into the parking lot, a car screeched around the corner.

They jumped back up onto the steps, Lexy's heart leaping into her throat when the car careened past, barely missing them as it sped off toward the exit. She'd had just enough time to look inside at the driver.

"Did you see who that was?" Nans asked.

Lexy nodded. "Ramona—and she was driving a red Toyota Corolla."

Chapter Sixteen

Lexy was just leaving the retirement center after dropping Nans and the gang off when her cell phone made cooing dove noises—her ringtone for Jack.

"Hi," she chirped into the phone.

"Hey there." Jack's deep baritone caressed her ear and Lexy's pulse quickened. Her lips curled up in a smile—his voice still affected her the same way it had when they'd first met. "I heard you caused a little trouble over at McGreevey's."

Lexy cringed. "Hey, that wasn't my fault. Ramona started it."

Jack laughed. "Well, I'm sure you and Nans were there for reasons other than paying your condolences. How 'bout we meet for dinner and you can tell me what you found out."

"Dinner?" Lexy glanced at the clock, surprised to discover it was after five o'clock.

"Yeah, you don't have plans with your folks or anything, do you?" Jack asked.

"No, they're having dinner with some old friends tonight. I'm free."

"Great. Meet me at *The Burger Barn* in ten."

"Okay. See you then." Lexy snapped the phone shut. She was excited at the thought of meeting Jack at their favorite restaurant. Things had been so crazy lately she hadn't been able to spend much time with him, and her parents' presence in her driveway pretty much eliminated any possibility of spending any time alone with him.

She pulled into *The Burger Barn* a few minutes later. Jack was already there so she pulled her little Beetle up next to his truck. Jack jumped out of his truck and came over to open the door for her.

"Wow, you look great." He held her at arm's length and made a big show of looking her up and down. Lexy giggled as he let out a wolf whistle.

Jack brushed his lips against her forehead, his hands on her shoulders. "How was your day?"

"Great." Her five-foot-one frame made it necessary for her to tilt her head back to look up at all six feet of him. "How about you?"

"Good, but I'm starved. Let's eat." He draped his arm around her shoulders as they walked to the entrance. The smell of grilling meat hung in the air and Lexy's stomach grumbled. She hadn't realized how hungry she was ... a burger sure would hit the spot.

They got a seat in their favorite booth and ordered right away. Neither one of them needed to see a menu. They'd eaten there enough times to have it memorized.

"How are things going with your dress? Is it going to be ready?" Jack asked over the rim of his beer.

"Dress?" Lexy's brows mashed together as she stared blankly at Jack.

"Yeah, you know—your wedding dress? You do remember that we are getting married Saturday, don't you?" Jack teased.

Lexy slapped her forehead with her palm. "Yes, of course. I guess I've been so focused on this investigation I hadn't been thinking about the dress, but my mom has it all under control."

Lexy started mentally going over her "to-do" list for the wedding.

What else had she forgotten?

Her stomach fluttered with nerves as she pictured the ceremony without flowers or the reception without food because she'd forgotten to finalize some detail ... like making sure the guys got fitted for tuxes.

"What about the tuxes?" she asked.

"All taken care of." Jack smiled. "Your dad and I went downtown and got fitted today. Then we hung out at the cigar club and had a few beers."

Lexy frowned into her beer—she'd been so immersed in the murders that she didn't even know Jack had taken her dad out for some male bonding.

"Gosh, I've been so busy with this investigation. I haven't been paying attention to much else." Lexy put her hand over Jack's hand. "I'm sorry."

He flipped his hand over and laced his fingers with hers. “No worries. I don’t blame you for investigating it. I’ve been keeping an eye on it for you and Davies isn’t doing a half-bad job.”

“Really? She seems like a total ditz to me.”

Jack laughed and leaned back in his chair. “I did find out something about the case today that you might be interested in.”

Lexy lifted her brow slightly. “Spill it.”

“The medical examiner nailed down the time of death for all three victims. Stuart Wiggins died *before* Veronica and Philippe. *And* they were all shot with the same gun.”

Lexy chewed her bottom lip. “So he didn’t kill her.”

“Nope.” Jack pushed his beer aside to make room for the plate the waitress was setting on the table. Lexy did the same, taking the top bun off her burger so she could smother it in ketchup. She replaced the bun and brought the burger to her lips, opening her mouth as wide as she could in order to fit it into her mouth.

The melded flavors of beef, cheese, ketchup, pickles and mayo tickled her taste buds and she leaned back in her seat and thought about Jack’s news while she chewed.

If Stuart didn't kill Veronica in a fit of anger, then who did? Who was the target at *Chez Philippe*? Philippe, Veronica ..., or both of them? She shook her head as she swallowed the bite.

"This doesn't make any sense. I thought for sure Stuart killed her because of the fight they had." She took the top of the bun off of her burger and cut into it with her knife and fork. The burger was so thick that she always ended up eating it this way, even though she usually made at least one attempt to eat it with her hands.

"It looks like someone wanted both of them dead." Jack dipped a french fry into the puddle of ketchup he'd poured on his plate. "Do you have any idea why someone would want that?"

Lexy shook her head. "No, but I did find out who has the red Toyota."

"The one that Wiggins' neighbor thought he saw Veronica driving?"

"Yes. We saw Veronica's best friend, Ramona, driving one today at the funeral home." Lexy shoveled a pickle, piece of the bun and a piece of the burger onto her fork, balancing it precariously on the way to her mouth.

Jack pressed his lips together. "Maybe Veronica borrowed it that day ... or it could have been Ramona that had the fight with Stuart."

"I hadn't thought about that. But now that you mention it, Ramona and Veronica do look kind of alike. They have the same hair color and style."

"You might want to dig around and see how well Ramona and Stuart got along," Jack said.

Lexy made a face. "Well, I won't be asking Ramona. She practically punched me out at the wake and then almost ran us over with her car."

Jack took a sip of beer. "Well, it certainly is a perplexing case."

"Yeah, and I feel like *I'm* Davies best suspect. If *you're* perplexed, then imagine how she must feel." Lexy pushed the rest of her burger away. "That's why I need to be on top of this investigation with Nans and the ladies ... and I need dessert."

Jack laughed. "The usual?"

Lexy nodded. They always split a piece of double chocolate cake. Jack signaled the waitress and put in the order asking for an extra plate and fork.

"So how is the investigation going with Nans? Do you have any leads?"

Lexy made a face. "Not really. We have a few more things to check on. We did discover that Philippe had a large sum of money deposited to his personal bank account a while back. I'm not sure if Davies knows that, and I don't want to tell her because I have a sneaky suspicion Ruth doesn't exactly follow all the usual legal channels to get that sort of information."

"That could be important to the case ... sounds like Philippe might have been involved in something." Jack paused as the waitress brought the cake over. "Maybe the killer was really after *him* and Veronica just happened to be in the wrong place at the wrong time."

"Yeah, but then who shot Stuart?" Lexy plunged her fork into the gooey dessert, careful to get a good amount of frosting along with the moist cake.

"Good question." Jack sat back in his seat and watched Lexy polish off the rest of the cake. "I'm sure Nans and the ladies will come up with something. In the meantime, let's keep each other posted about anything new that crops up. I may not be officially on the case, but I still have some influence at the police department."

"Sounds good." Lexy smiled. She felt a lot more confident about the police finding the real killer now that she knew Jack had his eye on the case. "I just hope things get settled before this weekend, or we may be getting married in a jail cell."

Jack laughed as he stood and threw some money on the table for the bill. "I don't think things are that bad. I'm sure Davies doesn't really suspect you."

Lexy raised a brow at him as they walked toward the door. Judging by what Davies had said to her in the funeral home, she was at the top of the list.

Outside, it was a typical fall night with a bright full moon and a crisp chill in the air. Leaves crunched under their feet as they walked to their cars. Lexy shivered, rubbing her bare arms to generate warmth.

"Are you cold?" Jack put his arm around her and she snuggled into the warmth of his body.

"Yeah. This sleeveless shirt seemed like a good idea in the afternoon when it was eighty degrees. I didn't know I was going to be out after dark." Lexy laughed. Then her voice turned serious. "Plus I'm a little nervous about going back to my house, what with the break-in last night and all."

Jack stopped at her car door and turned her to face him. "I figured you might be, so I'm going to follow you home and come inside with you. I want to make sure the house is secure and you feel safe."

Lexy's heart flooded with warmth. "Thanks."

Jack traced her bottom lip with his thumb and Lexy felt a flurry of tingles in her belly. Her pulse skittered as he lowered his head, his lips brushing against hers—gently at first and then deeper, more insistent. Just when she thought her knees would turn to jelly, he broke the kiss.

“And, if you don’t feel safe there by yourself tonight, I’ll be more than happy to stay,” he said with a knowing smile as he reached behind her to open the car door.

Chapter Seventeen

Lexy dreamed she was on the beach. The ocean made soothing lapping sounds on the sugar white sand as the sun warmed her back. She rolled over to face Jack who was lying on the blanket beside her, his muscular body tanned from lazy days lying in the tropical sun.

Jack smiled at her, playfully pushing the side of her yellow bikini bottom down on her hip just a quarter inch to reveal her tan line.

"I'd like to see more of these tan lines," he said.

Lexy was just about to reply with a "yes" when she heard her mother yelling from further down the beach.

"Lexy ... Yoo-hoo. Time to get up!"

Get up? Lexy looked down the beach, her mood deflating when she saw her mother hurrying toward them dragging a wheeled cart stacked with a cooler, blankets and beach towels.

"Leeexxyy!"

Lexy jerked awake. She wasn't on the beach, but Jack *was* beside her. And her mother really was yelling.

She jumped out of the bed and ran to the window. Vera was standing in the front yard, hand shading her eyes as she peered up at the house.

"Yoo-hoo!" Vera waved, shouting loud enough to wake up the neighbors.

Lexy pushed the window open. "Just a minute Mom, I'll be right down to let you in."

She turned in a panic toward Jack who was sitting up in the bed. "You have to get out of here, my mom's coming in."

Jack laughed as he pushed the covers aside and stood. Lexy would have normally taken that opportunity to admire his muscular body but the close proximity of her naked fiancé to her mother outside the door made her panic.

"Lexy, we're getting married in two days, I'm sure your mother knows that we ..." He gestured toward the bed, which was rumpled from the night's activities.

Lexy picked up his clothes that were heaped in a pile on the floor and shoved them at him. "Just put these on and go out the back door. I'll call you later."

She ran to her bureau and picked out the first sweatshirt and sweatpants she could find, threw them on, and then ran downstairs pushing Jack in front of her.

He took a left into the kitchen while Lexy raced over to the front door, waiting until she heard the sound of the kitchen door shutting in the back before she opened it.

"What brings you out so early, Mom?" Lexy stared at her mother whose bright yellow sweat suite was only partially obscured by the mounds of satin and lace she had piled up in her arms. Lexy thought she recognized her wedding dress, along with a bright fuchsia silk fabric that she prayed her mother hadn't decided to embellish her dress with.

"It's such a beautiful day." Vera practically sang as she looked up at the sky. "Blue skies, and look at the trees! They'll be a gorgeous backdrop for your wedding pictures."

Lexy poked her head outside. There was still an early morning chill in the air, but the scenery was worth it. It was peak foliage season and the trees made a breathtaking display with their red, yellow and orange leaves. It *was* going to make a perfect backdrop for her wedding pictures ... exactly as she planned. She just hoped Davies didn't haul her off in handcuffs before she got to the wedding.

"It's gorgeous," Lexy said looking back at the pile of fabric in her mother's hand. "What have you got there?"

"I brought over your wedding dress for a fitting and I wanted to show off the dress I'm going to wear. I made it special for the occasion." Vera beamed with pride.

Lexy pushed the door wide. "Well, then come on in."

Vera laid the dresses carefully on Lexy's sofa. "I have your dress almost finished, but I only basted in the stitching. I'll fit it to you today, and do the final stitching tonight. It will be finished tomorrow!"

"Perfect." Lexy admired the dress, thankfully, her mother hadn't added any garish embellishments—it was exactly as she had designed it.

"Should we go upstairs?" Vera looked at the big picture window. "I'm not sure you want everyone looking in while you are half-dressed."

Lexy pictured the rumpled bed in her room. "I'll just run up and make the bed—why don't you make us a couple of teas in the kitchen and come right up?"

"Good idea." Vera bustled off toward the kitchen and Lexy picked up the dresses and ran upstairs. She was just tightening the comforter under the pillows when Vera joined her with two steaming mugs of tea.

Lexy laid the dresses out on the bed. Her mother's was a gorgeous color, but Lexy couldn't make out the style. It looked like it had an oversized collar and a full skirt.

"Your dress is so pretty, Mom. Why don't you try it on first and then we'll get to work on mine."

"Okay." Vera handed Lexy the mugs of tea and picked up her dress with the enthusiasm of a schoolgirl trying on a prom dress. "I'll just be right back."

Lexy put Vera's mug on the bureau and sat on the bed while she sipped her tea. After a few minutes, Vera emerged from the bathroom in a whirl of pink. The gown was vintage Vera—bright in color and a little offbeat in style. It had a mid-calf length full skirt that was shorter in the front and longer in the back. The waist and bust were tightly fitted. Cap sleeves covered her shoulders and an over exaggerated collar fanned around the back of her head, sticking stiffly up about six inches like something from the Elizabethan times. It was an odd gown, but somehow on Vera, it worked.

"That looks gorgeous, Mom," Lexy said. "You made that?"

"Yep." Vera twirled around to show off the dress, snuck a peak at herself in Lexy's full-length mirror then clapped her hands together. "Okay, enough about me. Put your dress on while I change out of this. Be careful—don't pull on the seams, they're only basted."

Vera disappeared back into the bathroom and Lexy took off her sweat suit then slipped into the gown. Standing in front of the mirror, she admired the gorgeous beading and rhinestones. Smoothing it across her midsection, she noticed it wasn't quite as tight—and the bust seemed to fit better. Maybe the dress being ripped was a blessing in disguise, her mother had done a great job with the alterations and now it was a perfect fit.

Vera came back out in the yellow sweat suit, her fuchsia dress hanging over her arm. "Oh that looks gorgeous on you." Mother and daughter smiled at each other in the mirror and Lexy's heart warmed. Vera might be a little unusual, but Lexy loved her.

"Okay," Vera said producing a sewing kit out of the middle pocket of her hoodie. "Stand still and I'll make sure it's just perfect.

Lexy did as she was told while Vera tugged and pulled at the dress. Vera nodded, then opened the sewing kit and took out some long pins. Lexy held her breath, waiting to get stuck.

"So, tell me about this whole murder business with your dressmaker," Vera mumbled around the pins she was holding between her lips. "Are you somehow involved?"

"Oh that?" Lexy said. "I'm not really *involved,* but he did design the dress. I was supposed to talk to him about repairing the tears in the dress that night ... the night he was killed."

Vera stood back and frowned at Lexy. "Just how *did* the dress get ripped, anyway?"

Lexy's cheeks burned. "I kind of got into a fight with another bride whose dress was similar."

Vera took the last pin out of her mouth and burst out laughing. "You did? I can't picture that—seems like something Nans would do though, maybe you're starting to take after her."

Vera walked behind Lexy and did more pulling and tugging, then reached for more pins. "So, if you're not involved in it, then why did someone break in here?"

"I don't know. For all we know that wasn't even related," Lexy said. "It could have just been a random break in"

Vera pulled the dress tight and stuck in a pin, almost jabbing Lexy. "Well, I think I know who did it anyway."

Lexy twisted around to look at her mother. "You do?"

"Yep. Last night we had dinner with the Stottlemeyer's. And Philippe's seamstress, Millie, is Georgia's aunt."

Lexy raised a brow at her mother. "And?"

"She said that Millie has been acting very strange for a month or so now," Vera said.

"Strange, how?"

"Evasive ... Nervous. That's exactly how someone who is up to no good acts. And they said she's not normally like that at all." Vera put in the last pin and stood back to inspect the dress. "I'd bet my right eye tooth she's got something to do with the murders."

Chapter Eighteen

"So, should we move Millie over to the suspects list?" Ruth stood in front of the whiteboard, her blue marker poised to write. Lexy looked at Nans—she wasn't sure how reliable Vera's information was.

"Well, she *was* acting very strange when Lexy, Ida and I saw her at *Chez Philippe*," Nans said. "We might as well put her under the suspects and make a note to question her again."

"We can cross Wiggins off. He was killed first, so he couldn't have killed the others," Lexy added.

"And since they were all killed with the same gun, the killer probably wasn't Veronica." Ida leaned against the entry from the dining room to the living room with a mug of coffee in her hand."

"Unless she killed Wiggins then someone took the gun from her and killed her and Philippe," Helen added.

Nans pressed her lips together. "I suppose that's possible, but since she's dead we can't question her. That leaves Millie, Ramona and Eddie."

"Ramona sure did act strange at the wake," Ida said.

"Well, that could have just been because she hates me. But I do have to admit I wouldn't feel too bad if she were the killer." Lexy chewed on her bottom lip. "In fact, that Eddie guy seemed to imply that she was up to something."

"We need to talk to both her and Millie," Nans said, then turned to Ruth. "Did you find out where that big payment Philippe got came from?"

Ruth shook her head. "It was a cash deposit so I can't trace it."

Nans tapped her fingers on her lips. "Hmm ... well somewhere, someone has fifty grand less money. Did you check the accounts of the other people involved?"

"Yep. The only one that had any significant amount of money going in and out was Wiggins. But he didn't withdraw that much at any one time," Ruth said. "Of course I only checked the last two months. Maybe I should look back further."

"Yes, do that," Nans said. "In the meantime, I think we need to pay a little visit to Millie over at *Chez Philippe*."

***

Lexy and Nans decided to go to *Chez Philippe* alone. Millie might be more apt to talk if she wasn't overwhelmed by five people. As they walked to Lexy's car, she noticed a black sedan idling at the end of the parking lot. The hairs on the back of her neck prickled.

Was the person in the car watching them?

"Is something wrong?" Nans asked.

"No. I think I'm just getting paranoid with the murders and the break-in." Lexy laughed. "I'm starting to think people are after me."

Nans narrowed her eyes at the black car. "Which brings up the question ... why *did* someone break into your house?"

"That's been bugging me too," Lexy said as they got into her car. "The only thing I can think of is maybe they think I have whatever Philippe got paid the fifty grand for."

"Indeed," Nans said.

They drove the short distance to *Chez Philippe* in silence. When they got there, they could see the lights on in the showroom.

"Looks like it's open," Nans said as Lexy drove by. She pulled into an empty spot a couple of doors down and they got out.

"Now, let me do all the talking," Nans said as they approached the door. "I know just what to say."

"If you say so." Lexy opened the door and they entered the empty shop.

"Hello. Anyone here?" Nans called.

"I'm in the back." Millie's voice answered from the back room of the shop.

Nans motioned to Lexy and they walked over to the back room, both of them entering through the wide doorway at the same time.

Millie was sitting at a sewing table stitching lace onto a piece of white fabric by hand. She held the fabric up about an inch from her face. She squinted over at them as they entered, not recognizing them at first until her eyes adjusted. Then, once she realized who they were, her eyes widened.

"*You* people again." She sighed. "What do you want now?"

"We're investigating the murders and we want to ask you some questions," Nans said, as if they were "officially" investigating.

Millie straightened her back. "I've already talked to the police."

"Some new things have come to light since then and we have more questions." Nans walked closer to Millie. "You weren't here that night, right?"

"Like I said *before*, I went out to get coffees. Philippe ... Mr. Montague ... was meeting with Ms. Veronica. I went down to *Fresh Market* to get Mr. Montague's favorite cinnamon roll and then over to Starbucks for coffees." Millie looked like she was about to tear up, then her eyes turned cold when she looked at Lexy. "One might wonder what *you* were doing here."

"I was supposed to meet with Philippe ... about fixing my dress," Lexy said.

"Oh, but I thought you ripped Ms. Veronica's dress?" Millie narrowed her eyes at Lexy.

"She ripped mine! ... Well and I guess I ripped hers, too. She was mad because they were so similar."

Millie looked away. Lexy thought she almost looked guilty, which made her wonder if the similarity of the dresses was a mistake or not.

Nans continued her interrogation. "Were you and Mr. Montague up to something?"

Millie's hands jerked, the needle dug into her finger. "Ouch!" She pulled her hand away and shoved her finger in her mouth.

"Whatever gave you that idea?" she mumbled around her finger while glaring at Nans.

"We know something was going on ... we just don't know what." Nans started walking around the room. "Unless you want us to guess the worst, I suggest you come out with it."

"How dare you!" Millie stood up, knocking the sewing from the table then bending down to retrieve it, obviously flustered.

Nans showed no mercy and swooped in for the kill. "We have statements from witnesses that know about it."

Millie collapsed in her chair and sobbed into her hands.

"It's all too much," She blurted out in-between sobs.

Nans rushed to her side and rubbed her arm. Lexy found the box of tissues and shoved them toward her.

"What's too much? What was going on with Philippe?" Nans asked.

"We were having an affair!" Millie blurted out. "I'm so ashamed.

"Ashamed? But neither of you are married so what's to be ashamed about?"

"Well, a woman of my age? Taking up with a man?" Millie's cheeks flushed. "In my day, that just wasn't done."

Lexy and Nans exchanged a glance.

"That's *it*? That's what you've been so nervous about?" Lexy asked.

Millie nodded then said softly, "That and the dresses."

"The dresses? What about them?" Nans asked soothingly.

"Well, you see I'm getting on in years. My eyesight and creativity isn't what it used to be ... so, sometimes, I design similar dresses to make it easier on myself." She looked at Lexy apologetically. "That's what happened with your dress and Ms. Veronica's."

"Where did the money come from?" Nans asked.

"Money?" Millie looked from Nans to Lexy. "What money?"

"Surely you noticed that Philippe came into a large sum of money a few months ago?"

Millie's eyes narrowed. "That's not true. Philippe didn't mention anything ... and I'm sure he would have told me."

"It's true. Did you notice he was acting strange the past few months?"

"Well, he was acting kind of strange lately ... distant." Millie looked down at her hands in her lap. "I was worried that he'd tired of me."

"Are you sure you don't know anything about the money?" Nans persisted. "We think that whatever he was involved in was what got him killed, so if you know something, it would be in your best interest to tell us now."

Millie held her hands up. "I don't know a thing, I swear!"

Nans nodded and stood up. She took a few paces into the middle of the room then turned around to face Millie again.

"If you don't know anything about the money, then didn't you wonder *who* would have murdered Philippe and *why*?"

Millie glanced sideways at Lexy. "Well to tell you the truth, when I saw Ms. Baker here that night, I thought she killed them both over the dress. It made perfect sense ... the two girls fought earlier in the day and I was certain they were both mad as hens to have discovered their dresses were almost identical."

"Seriously? You don't think Lexy would kill over something like that, do you?" Nans waved her hand at Lexy.

Millie snorted. "Believe me. I've seen brides do all kinds of things when it comes to their dresses."

"I can assure you, I didn't kill them," Lexy said. "In fact, I think whoever *did* kill them might be after me. That's why we're so interested in finding them."

"Oh dear. That's terrible," Millie said.

"Yes, so if you think of anything that could help us ... maybe something Philippe said, or something you saw at the shop, please let me know." Nans pulled out her *Ladies Detective Club* business card and handed it to Millie.

Lexy and Nans turned to leave and Millie called out behind them. "I'm truly sorry about the gowns, Lexy."

Lexy turned to face the other woman. Millie looked so sad, Lexy didn't have it in her to be mad and, besides, her gown was perfect. "That's okay, Millie. I love the gown and who cares if it's similar to another one anyway?"

"Oh thank you for being so understanding," Millie said as Lexy turned back to leave. "You're so much nicer than that *other* girl that asked about the gowns."

Nans and Lexy spun around and spoke at the same time. "Other girl?"

"Yes, that friend of Ms. Veronica's ... what was her name ...?" Millie tapped her lips with her index finger.

"Ramona?" Lexy asked.

"Yes, that's it. She was here asking about Ms. Veronica's dress. An impertinent young miss she was too. Nasty girl." Millie made a sour face.

"What was she asking?" Nans asked.

"Oh, where the dress was and so on." Millie waved her hand. "I told her I had no idea where it was. Ms. Veronica must have it at home somewhere as it certainly isn't here. She stormed out of here and nearly broke the door slamming it so hard."

"Young people these days," Nans said shaking her head. "Well, thanks for your time, and please do let me know if you remember anything that might be connected to this mess."

"Will do," Millie said.

Nans took Lexy by the arm and practically ran her out of the building into the car. Once she was seated, she whipped her iPad out of her purse and started typing like a mad woman.

"What are you doing?" Lexy asked.

"Sending a message to Ruth ... I need her to find out everything she can about this Ramona person. And we need to get back to my place pronto ... I think we might be getting close to solving this case."

Chapter Nineteen

"I know Ramona has something to do with this," Nans said once they were back in her apartment with Ida, Ruth and Helen. "Did you find anything Ruth?"

"I didn't have much time to search on her, Mona ... I mean you only called like fifteen minutes ago."

"Oh, sorry. Sometimes I get carried away." Nans gave a sheepish shrug.

"But I *did* find something interesting about Stuart Wiggins." Ruth's eyes twinkled.

"You did?"

"Yep. It seems he's been getting credit card advances over the past three months. That money doesn't appear in his bank account ... and it all adds up to just a little over fifty thousand dollars."

"He could have used it to pay for wedding stuff," Lexy said picturing her own mounting wedding expenses.

"True." Ruth nodded. "But I also discovered that he and Ramona went to the same college in Texas ... and guess who else went there?"

Lexy, Nans, Ida and Helen stared at her. Finally, Helen said, "I give up ... who?"

"Eddie Sharp."

"What did Ramona go to college for?" Lexy wondered.

"Computer Technology," Ruth said. "She barely graduated. It says here she works at the museum too."

"So, all three of them went to college together and got jobs at the same place." Ida shrugged. "So what? Lots of people remain friends for years after college and recommend their friends for jobs at their place of employment."

"It does make sense that Veronica could have met Stuart through Ramona. Lots of people introduce their friends to each other," Helen pointed out.

"So, maybe Stuart was into something with Philippe and that's why they were both killed. Veronica might just have been in the wrong place and got killed along with Philippe," Lexy said.

"Or Veronica was in on it too and the killer wanted all three of them dead," Ida added.

"Yes, but *what* were they into and *who* killed them?" Nans asked.

"I don't know," Lexy said as she stood up. "But I think finding the money trail is a job for the police and I'm pretty sure all this evidence lets me off the hook. In fact, I'm going to call Jack as soon as I get home and let him know."

"But what about Ramona?" Nans asked.

"She's just mean," Lexy said. "Always was in school, too. Her behavior might seem suspicious, but for her, acting like that is normal."

"Does that mean you don't want to come with me to interrogate her tomorrow?" Nans looked crestfallen.

"Sorry, Nans. It's the day before my wedding and I have a ton to do." Lexy felt a tug at her heart—she hated to disappoint Nans but she *did* have a lot of last minute errands to run. "Besides, it seems like the case is pretty much solved. Davies just needs to connect the money between Wiggins and Philippe and find the other person involved and she'll have her killer."

Lexy was halfway to the door before Ida's voice stopped her. "Wait a minute. If it's as you say ... then why did someone break into your house?"

Lexy's brow creased.

She turned around. "That's a good question. I guess they must think I have something ... although I can't imagine what. I'm sure the police will figure that all out once you give them this information you found."

"Well, you better be careful, dear," Nans said. "The killer is loose out there and he may still think you have something he needs."

***

Lexy pushed away the niggle of doubt that clutched at her as she pulled out of the *Brooke Ridge Falls Retirement Center*. Nans and the ladies had found compelling evidence that Stuart Wiggins and Philippe were into something together and she could trust the police to come to the right conclusion. *Couldn't she?*

She thought about Davies and wondered if she was competent enough to figure the rest of it out.

Well, she'll just have to be, Lexy thought, because she didn't have time to continue an investigation herself right now.

Her heart flooded with warmth as she thought about her wedding. *Hers and Jack's wedding*. It was going to be beautiful. The weather was supposed to be sunny and in the seventies. The leaves were in full color and she'd be wearing her gorgeous dress. If she could tie up some of the loose ends tomorrow and make it to the rehearsal dinner, everything would be perfect.

She pulled up in front of her house and walked to the front door, her stomach clenching as she put the key in the lock. She was still a little spooked about the break-in and apprehensive about what she might find inside.

She took a deep breath and shoved the key in. It's no good being afraid of walking into your own home, she thought as she shoved the door open. Her breath came out in a whoosh of relief—the house was exactly as she left it.

"Lexy! Is that you?" Vera's voice echoed across the entire neighborhood.

She turned and poked her head out the door to see Vera running across the lawn, her arms loaded with mail, Sprinkles racing along beside her.

"Hi Mom," Lexy said.

"I got your mail ... the box was overflowing." Vera handed Lexy the pile.

"I guess I must have forgotten about it, the past couple of days have been so busy," Lexy said grabbing the mail. "Come on in."

Lexy felt exhausted. The stress of the past few days was catching up with her. She collapsed on the couch, throwing the mail on the coffee table. Sprinkles jumped up beside her and she hugged the small dog, her heart surging at her unconditional love. Giving the dog a kiss on the head, she turned her attention to the mail.

"Let's see what's in here." She sorted through the pile, throwing each piece down on the table after she looked at it. "Bills, bills, bills, catalog, letter ..."

"Why are there always so many bills and never any checks?" Vera joked.

"I know." Lexy laughed. "Well none of this needs immediate attention." She frowned at the letter. She didn't recognize the handwriting or the name on the return address. Probably someone sending her wedding wishes.

"You look exhausted," Vera said. "I have some beef stew cooking in the crock pot, why don't you come over and eat with us?"

"That would be great, Mom."

"Oh good." Vera clapped her hands. "We only have a few more days together until you go on your honeymoon and we take off again in the big rig, and we want to see as much of you as we can."

"Me too." Lexy got up and hugged her mother as they started out the door. She was careful to close it and lock it before turning to follow her mother to the RV. She was just starting across the lawn with Sprinkles running circles around her ankles when something at the end of the street caught her eye.

Her stomach lurched–was that the tail end of a black car disappearing around the corner?

Lexy hesitated then realized she was just being paranoid. How many black cars were there in Brooke Ridge Falls? It was probably just one of the neighbors driving home. She followed Vera into the RV, stopping at the door to cast one last nervous glance over her shoulder, to make sure the street was empty before she went inside.

Chapter Twenty

Lexy plumped her pillow and rolled over to face the windows. The sun streaming in through the leaves on the big oak tree out front created a kaleidoscope of light on her floor and bedspread.

It was going to be another beautiful day. Lexy smiled as she reached under the covers to pet Sprinkles. Today was the day before her wedding and, now that the messy triple murder was soon to be resolved, she could relax and focus on starting her new life as Mrs. Jack Perillo. Which meant she better get going—she had to run some last minute errands or there might not *be* a wedding tomorrow.

She jumped into the shower, and then changed into a pair of comfy jeans and a plain black tee-shirt. Tying her hair in a ponytail, she grabbed her white hoodie, put Sprinkles into her harness and then headed out the door with the little dog at her side.

Lexy drove downtown, glancing every few minutes in the rear-view mirror. She was still a little spooked by the black car she *thought* she kept seeing, but no one followed her. Maybe Davies had already arrested the killer.

"Are you ready for a spa treatment?" Lexy asked Sprinkles as she pulled up in front of the *Pretty*

Paws dog grooming. Sprinkles looked out the window then eyed Lexy dubiously. Clearly, the dog was not fooled by the word 'spa'.

Lexy got out of the car and came around to the passenger side to collect Sprinkles. She opened the door and tugged on the leash. Sprinkles hopped out grudgingly.

"You're gonna like this Sprinks. I promise," Lexy said as she pulled to dog into the groomers.

Lexy handed Sprinkles over to the girl behind the desk and walked out to the sidewalk, enjoying the sun warming her shoulders. It was already seventy degrees–she wouldn't need her hoodie today. She unzipped the sweatshirt and threw it into her car, then opted to walk the three blocks to the caterer where she finalized the appetizer selection and gave the menu her final approval.

She took her time on the way back, looking in the shop windows. She spotted a Gucci bag she would have loved, but couldn't quite afford. She stopped in front of the chocolatier, her mouth watering at the fancy chocolates in the window and the smell of rich chocolate that filled the air.

She was debating on whether she should buy a hunk of almond bark when she saw the reflection of a black car in the window. Her heart froze and she whirled around just in time to see it disappearing around the corner.

Was it the same car she'd seen before?

She hadn't gotten a good enough look to be sure but she hurried back to the safety of her car anyway. Sitting inside, she adjusted the rear view mirror to look at the traffic. After a few minutes with no black car in sight, she relaxed.

Probably just my overactive imagination.

She glanced at her watch. With two more hours until she could pick up Sprinkles, now was the perfect time to check in at the bakery. She pulled out of her parking spot and pointed her car toward The Cup and Cake.

***

"So Davies doesn't think you're the killer anymore?" Cassie asked after Lexy had filled her in on the information the ladies had dug up.

"Well, she hasn't exactly *said* as much, but since she hasn't arrested me, I feel pretty confident that she's ruled me out." Lexy poured herself a french vanilla coffee from the self-serve station in the café section of *The Cup and Cake,* then sat down at the table across from Cassie. The girls had spent the last two hours baking a batch of pies and were now taking a well-deserved break.

"But the killer still thinks you know something ... or have something, right?" Cassie narrowed her eyes at Lexy over the steaming mug of herbal tea she held up to her lips.

Lexy looked across the street at the falls. The soothing motion of the cascading water contrasted with the feeling of uneasiness that was creeping into her chest. "I'm not sure. I have no idea what they were looking for in there."

Cassie's phone chirped and she dug for it in her pocket. "It's a text from John. Let me text him back and see if he knows anything about the case."

Lexy sipped her coffee while Cassie used her thumbs to message John. A few seconds later, her phone chirped again.

"No one has been arrested," Cassie said.

"Do they have any suspects?" Lexy asked.

Cassie thumb typed into her phone again, then set it on the table and took a bite of the cannoli she'd swiped from the case.

The phone chirped again and Cassie picked it up. "He says he doesn't know if there are any suspects but he said he heard Davies say something about putting a tail on *you*."

Lexy's brow creased. *Was it Davies in the black car she kept seeing?*

"That's crazy, why would they want to follow me?" Lexy asked.

Cassie shrugged. "Maybe she thinks you are going to lead her to a clue ... or incriminate yourself somehow."

"Incriminate myself? But I didn't do anything!"

"Well *you* know that and *I* know that, but Davies ... I'm not so sure what she knows."

Lexy chewed on her bottom lip and tapped her finger on the glass tabletop. What if Davies still thought she was involved and arrested her before the wedding ... or told her she couldn't leave town on her honeymoon? Perhaps she'd been too hasty in assuming Nans' information would give Davies what she needed to arrest the real killer.

She stared out the window at the falls. The sun was just at the right angle so that it reflected like jewels off the rushing water. With a start, Lexy realized it was late afternoon. She pushed herself away from the table.

"I better get going. I have to pick up Sprinkles at the groomers and then go home and get ready for the rehearsal dinner."

"Rehearsal dinner? Oh, is that tonight?" Cassie scrunched her brow and tilted her head at Lexy.

Lexy had a moment of panic ... then realized her friend was teasing. "Very funny. You and John will be there, right? I mean you are the maid of honor and best man."

"Of course," Cassie said. "Eight o'clock on the dot."

"Okay. See you then," Lexy said and then downed her coffee before rushing out the door to her car.

Chapter Twenty One

The reception area at *Pretty Paws* was packed full. Lexy tapped her foot impatiently while she waited for her turn. In front of her, a woman tried to keep the leashes of her two Yorkies from getting tangled as they zigzagged in between her legs. In front of the Yorkies, a man jerked the leash of his Golden Retriever to distract it from growling at the Great Dane that was in front of *him*.

Lexy had been taking Sprinkles to *Pretty Paws* for years now and she'd never seen it so crowded. Shannon, the harried woman at the reception desk, seemed like she could barely keep up.

"Are you giving away free grooming? I've never seen it so crowded here," Lexy said when it was finally her turn.

Shannon sighed, brushing wisps of hair that had escaped from her ponytail out of her face. "I know, it's been crazy. Guess I won't complain though because business is good." She frowned at Lexy. "What brings you back here?"

"I'm here to pick up Sprinkles. I dropped her off earlier, remember?"

"Yes, of course, but your sister picked her up about fifteen minutes ago."

Lexy's forehead pleated. "Sister? I don't have a sister. You must have me confused with someone else."

"Let me double check." Shannon rifled through some papers on the desk, pulling one out and handing it to Lexy.

"Yep, right here. Your sister Lavinia picked her up," she said as she motioned for the person behind Lexy to hand over their dogs.

Lexy frowned at the paper, her stomach sinking. *Lavinia? Who the heck was Lavinia?*

"No, really. I don't have a sister. This must be a mix-up." *Totally understandable given the chaos that was going on right now*, Lexy thought.

Shannon gave her an exasperated look as she tried to separate a Wheaton Terrier and Springer Spaniel that were having a spat.

"Honestly, Lexy. I distinctly remember handing Sprinkles to her. Medium height, fluffy dark hair. You can go back and check the kennels if you want." Shannon jerked her head toward the back of the store then turned her attention to the next customer.

Medium height? Fluffy dark hair?

An uneasy feeling crept into Lexy's stomach just as her cell phone went off. She yanked it out of her pocket. A number she didn't recognize flashed on the screen, but something told her to answer the call. She turned away from the reception desk and flipped the phone open.

"Hello?"

"Listen up, Baker. If you want to see your precious pooch alive, then do exactly as I say."

Lexy's heart twisted. She could hear Sprinkles barking in the background. "Who is this?"

The menacing laugh that came out of the phone chilled Lexy's blood. "Don't you recognize my voice? It's your old enemy ... and yes, that *is* Sprinkles you hear barking. Now, if you don't want her to get hurt, bring your wedding dress to six four three East Pearl at six-thirty p.m. Enter by the door on the side ... and come alone."

"My dress? Why would you want *that*?" Lexy's question was answered with the hollow click of the call being disconnected. But she'd recognized the voice and she knew who was on the other end. Ramona.

Panic gripped her as she shoved the phone back into her purse.

Sprinkles was in trouble!

She ran out to her car and called the first person she could think of to help—Nans.

***

Tears blurred Lexy's eyes as she looked through her cell phone contacts for Nans. Pressing the number, she could feel her heartbeat pounding with each ring. *Please answer.*

"Hi, Lexy I was jus—"

Lexy cut her off. "Ramona's kidnapped Sprinkles!"

Nans gasped. "What?"

"She pretended to be my sister and picked her up at the groomers," Lexy said.

"Why would she do that?"

"She wants me to bring my wedding dress to some building on the pier tonight. She says she'll hurt Sprinkles if I don't. What should I do?"

"Ahh. It all makes perfect sense now," Nans said. "Especially with what Millie just told me about the stones Philippe told her to sew into the gown."

"Huh? What stones? This doesn't make *any* sense to me," Lexy said feeling even more confused than before.

"Well I don't have time to explain it now," Nans said. "How quickly do you think Vera can sew up a wedding dress?"

Lexy felt her brows knit together. "I don't know. Why?"

"Because I have an idea on how we can catch our killer. But we'll have to hurry. We need to get Vera to work on the dress pronto *and* pay a visit to Detective Davies ... and we don't have much time."

Chapter Twenty Two

Lexy's heart hammered in her chest as she stood in front of 643 East Pearl Street clutching the wedding dress decoy her mother had made. East Pearl was in the seedy section of town, the streetlights had been smashed years ago and she could barely make out the numbers in the dim light.

Resisting the urge to run, she reached out for the knob and turned. The door opened into a dark warehouse.

"Hello?"

"Woof!"

"Sprinkles!" Lexy's heart surged and she ran toward the sound.

"So, you made it." The voice came from the shadows behind her and Lexy spun around. Two figures with guns stood in the corner.

"Bring the dress over," Ramona said.

"I want to see Sprinkles first," Lexy demanded.

A light flicked on at the far end and Lexy could see Sprinkles snuggled in a dog bed inside a large crate. Sprinkles thumped her tail against the side of the crate.

"She's fine," Ramona said. "Now give us what we want."

Lexy walked slowly over to the corner, her eyes slowly adjusting to the dim light. She sucked in a breath as the other person stepped out from behind Ramona.

"Eddie?"

"That's right; me and Eddie and Stu were all in on it together. Bet you and your nosey grandma didn't figure that one out," Ramona said. "Now hand over the dress."

She held the hand without the gun out and Lexy shoved the dress at her.

"What's so interesting about the dress?" Lexy asked, hoping that Ramona didn't inspect it too carefully—Vera hadn't had much time to make it and it was a barely passable copy of Lexy's gown.

"You didn't figure that out?" Ramona squinted at the top of the dress, and then held it up toward Lexy. "It's these stones. They aren't regular rhinestones—they're diamonds."

"Diamonds?"

"That's right," Eddie cut in. "We planned the heist at the Telbourne, and paid Philippe to sew the stones into Veronica's dress."

"Except we didn't know they were making an identical dress for you." Ramona glared at Lexy.

"And somehow the dresses got switched," Eddie said.

Lexy's brows creased. "So *that's* why my dress didn't fit as good on that last fitting."

"Right-o!" Ramona said.

"And you were all in on this together?" Lexy asked.

"Umm ... yeah, I think we already covered that," Ramona said.

"But why sew them into a dress?" Lexy asked.

"It was the easiest way to smuggle them out of the country," Eddie said. "With Stu and Veronica getting married in Paris, it was perfect ... Until Stu started trying to get more than his share."

"And that's why you killed him," Lexy said.

Eddie nodded. "And we had to take care of Philippe too. He knew too much. I just wish I didn't have to kill Veronica. She didn't know anything about it."

"Well, you dirty rotten scoundrels," Lexy said.

"What?" Ramona and Eddie both scrunched their faces at her.

"I said ... you dirty rotten scoundrels." Lexy repeated louder this time as she glanced behind her.

Where was Davies? Hadn't she said the right code words?

“Okay, now that we have the dress, what do we do with her?” Eddie jerked his head in Lexy’s direction.

Ramona’s laugh turned Lexy’s insides to mush.

“The joke’s on you Eddie,” Ramona said as she pointed her gun at him.

“What the heck?” Eddie pointed his gun at Ramona.

“I took the liberty of relieving your gun of its bullets,” Ramona said.

Lexy saw Eddie’s face turn hard and he squeezed the trigger. Lexy flinched but the gun only made a dull clicking sound. Ramona really *had* removed the bullets.

“I figured that with Stu out of the way, I might as well keep the profits for myself,” Ramona said.

“How are you going to do that?” Eddie asked.

“That’s easy.” Ramona gestured with her gun for Eddie to stand next to Lexy. “It turns out you couldn’t live without Lexy ... couldn’t stand to see her marry another man.”

“What?” Lexy asked. “No one is going to believe *that*—we didn’t even know each other until two days ago.”

“Oh, they’ll believe it.” Ramona snickered. “Especially once they get the letter Eddie sent to you saying that if he can't have you no one can, and begging you to meet him here."

Lexy remembered the strange letter she'd found in the previous night's mail and her stomach churned. Had Ramona really gone that far?

"Oh, and if they don't believe that, wait until they find your panties at Eddie's house and his necklace at yours."

Eddie looked down at his chest. "So that's where my necklace went—you took it!"

Ramona nodded.

"Wait. How'd you get my panties?"

"It was me that broke into your house," Ramona said proudly.

"You broke into my house to steal my panties?" Lexy stared at Ramona incredulously.

"Actually I broke in to get the dress, the panty stealing was just extra," Ramona said. "And, of course, I took the opportunity to plant the necklace."

"Now, all I have to do is make it look like Eddie killed you, then turned the gun on himself." Ramona shrugged. "Stuff like that happens all the time. *And* since I left the video tapes showing Eddie and Stu stealing that scepter at the Telbourne, the police will be so happy to catch their thieves *and* the killer they won't even look any further ... and I'll be on my way to Rio with the diamonds."

"You won't get away with this you dirty rotten scoundrel!" Lexy yelled the code words that Davies had given her.

Ramona shoved her into a corner and lifted the gun, the barrel pointing right at Lexy.

Lexy squeezed her eyes shut and covered her ears just before she heard a deafening bang.

***

"Hold it right there!" Lexy heard Davies yell. She opened one eye in time to see Ramona whirl around just as the Brooke Ridge Falls Police Department swarmed the room.

Before she could even get her other eye open, Davies had Ramona face down on the floor and was slapping handcuffs on her. John Darling was doing the same to Eddie. And Jack was scooping her up into his arms.

"Are you okay?" Lexy melted at the concern in his honey brown eyes.

Lexy nodded then tore herself out of his arms.

"Sprinkles!" She yelled, pointing to the corner the dog was in. Jack followed her over and they released the dog, all three of them falling into a group hug. Lexy scooped up Sprinkles and they walked back over to the group in time to hear Davies finish reading Eddie his rights.

"What took you guys so long to come in?" Lexy asked. "Did I get the code words wrong?"

"No, you got them right." Davies face flushed and she pulled on a piece of matted hair near her ear. "I got gum in my hair and must have missed hearing the signal at first."

Lexy raised a brow at Jack who shrugged.

"Well the important thing is that the killers are captured and now we can get married without any worries," he said draping his arm around Lexy's shoulders.

"Yeah, and now your new detective knows that I'm not a killer." Lexy stared at Davies.

"Oh, I knew you weren't the killer right from the get-go," Davies said. "I was just having some fun with you. Plus I wanted you and your grandmother to continue investigating—made my job a lot easier. Having you track down those leads was like having another team of detectives."

"So we helped you solve the case?" Nans asked from the doorway.

"Yes Ms. Baker, you sure did." Davies walked over to the doorway and gave Nans a hug. Lexy wondered when Nans had gotten so friendly with Davies.

"Umm ... that should be *cases*, shouldn't it?" Lexy said.

"That's right. You helped catch the people who stole the scepter from the museum *and* the killer of Stu, Philippe and Veronica," Jack said.

"Which reminds me." Davies looked at Lexy. "I'm going to need the real wedding dress. That thing has over five million dollars' worth of diamonds on it."

Lexy's stomach clenched. "My wedding dress?"

"Yep." Davies nodded. "It's evidence."

"But I'm getting married tomorrow, and I don't have anything else to wear!"

Chapter Twenty Three

Lexy stood at the altar facing Jack, her heart flooding with warmth at the loving look in his honey brown eyes. So far, everything had gone off without a hitch even though she'd almost missed her own rehearsal dinner the night before.

This morning, she'd arrived in her pink limo to find the church smothered in flowers and overflowing with guests. She'd had a few last minute jitters, which Cassie helped soothe *and* she'd had to fight back tears when her father walked her down the aisle and handed her over to Jack. But otherwise, everything was perfect.

And here she stood, next to Jack, in her five million dollar wedding gown.

Lexy glanced out at the guests. Her parents and Jack's parents sat in the front row proudly. Even Detective Davies had shown up and was sitting right up front in the second row. Lexy shot her a quick smile—the detective proved that she *did* have a heart when she let Lexy wear the wedding dress on the condition that she hand it over right after the wedding.

Lexy's smile faltered as she pictured Davies trying to rip the dress off her as soon as the reception ended. Davies did look cute though, in a tan suit with matching tan suede shoes. Lexy did a double take at the shoes.

Were those Jimmy Choo's?

Lexy leaned forward, to get a better look at Davies' shoes.

Was that a bloodstain on one of them? And if it was, how did Davies get her other shoe?

She frowned up at Davies who smiled and gave her a quick wink then brushed the leaf that Lexy mistook for a bloodstain from the tip of her shoe. Apparently, they had the same taste in shoes.

"Ahem ... Miss Baker?" The minister's voice caught her attention.

Lexy straightened and whipped her head back toward the minister. "Oh sorry. What?"

The minister looked back down at his book. "I was saying ... Do you take this man to be your lawfully wedded husband?"

Did she?

Lexy's heart fluttered in her chest as she suddenly realized the enormous commitment she was about to make.

She tried to picture them growing old together. What would that life be like? Did she want to spend the rest of her life with Jack?

Lexy looked over at Jack, then at the minister, then at all her guests. When she looked back at Jack again, she knew the answer.

She turned to the minister and said ...

"I do!"

Epilogue

"I guess there really is no honor among thieves," Nans said as she placed her coffee on the café table, pulled out a chair and sat down.

"Guess not." Lexy shrugged–she was still on a high from their wedding the day before and even the thought of the three murders couldn't dampen her spirits. Everything had gone perfectly at the reception and Cassie's cake had been both gorgeous and delicious. She had to admit she'd been a little nervous wearing the five million dollar gown and was glad to finally hand it over to Davies.

Now, sitting at the café tables at *The Cup and Cake* with her best friends and family, everything was perfect.

"I don't really understand how it all happened." Vera, in a bright turquoise and lime green outfit sat at the next table munching on a cinnamon roll.

"Stu, Ramona and Eddie planned the heist," Jack said. "Stu and Eddie arranged it so that they were the security detail at night and Ramona worked in the control room where they stored the videos from the security cameras. She removed the section of video that showed Stu and Eddie taking the scepter and replaced it with a section of tape from earlier but changed the time stamps."

“So it looked like the scepter was there one minute and then gone the next,” Nans added.

“Then they took the diamonds out of the scepter and Stu paid Philippe to have them sewn into Veronica’s gown,” John added. “Philippe’s business wasn’t doing well and I guess he took the money to try to save it.”

“It was almost perfect, except Millie switched the gowns by mistake during one of the fittings,” Nans said as she nibbled her éclair.

“And Stu got greedy, so Eddie and Ramona decided to cut him out,” Jack added. “That was Ramona that had the fight with Stu that day.”

“Eddie killed Stu and then went to get the gown,” John said. “I think Eddie expected *Chez Philippe* to be empty because the store is usually closed at that time, but when he got there, he found Philippe and Veronica—he shot them and took Veronica’s gown, which was actually the wrong one,” Jack went over to the self-serve coffee station to refill his cup.

“So, it was Eddie that broke into *Chez Philippe* the next night?” Lexy asked.

“Yes, at first we assumed the break-in was to cover up something about the murder, but he was actually looking for the stones. That’s why he ransacked the sewing area.”

Cassie narrowed her eyes. "So the whole time, Ramona was making plans to double-cross Eddie?"

"Yep." John nodded. "She'd already gotten him to do the killings, so all she had to do was make off with the stones, but when they discovered Eddie took the wrong gown, that screwed up her plan."

"And she *knew* I had a gown almost identical to Veronica's because she saw us that day at the fitting," Lexy said.

"Plus, she also knew you were doing some investigating," Nans added. "So once she figured out you had the dress with the real diamonds, she broke in to steal it from your house."

"Except it wasn't at Lexy's," Vera said. "I had it in the RV that we were driving around town in on that day."

"Right." Nans spooned some sugar into her coffee. "So, Ramona took the opportunity to plant the necklace she'd stolen from Eddie earlier and steal Lexy's red lace panties."

Lexy felt her cheeks grow warm. "Then later she planted the panties at Eddie's and wrote the fake note that she mailed to my house."

"We found those panties under Eddie's bed." Jack wiggled his eyebrows at Lexy whose cheeks got even warmer.

"And I think Eddie must have been working a plan to double-cross Ramona too," Nans said. "The few times we talked to him he kept trying to insinuate that Ramona was acting strange—he was trying to point us in her direction."

"And apparently he didn't tell Ramona he'd taken the dress ... not until after he discovered the stones weren't diamonds and he needed her help," John added.

"Well I'm just glad everything worked out, the case got solved, we got married and tomorrow we get to leave on our tropical honeymoon." Lexy smiled at Jack.

"Well, it's too bad you won't be around to see the new bakery go in across the street." Nans looked at the empty storefront almost directly across from The Cup and Cake.

Lexy froze. "What bakery?"

"Oh, you didn't hear?" Nans asked. "Someone is putting a bakery in just like The Cup and Cake right across the street. Isn't that stupid?"

Lexy looked out the window. It *did* look like someone was getting ready to move in to that empty store. But who would put a bakery right across from another bakery?

Cassie got up and stood right at the window squinting at the store. "It *is* stupid ... and it looks like they are painting it pink ... just like we have in here."

Lexy felt her heart squeeze. *Another bakery just like hers?* She didn't think she liked that idea much.

Jack squeezed her hand and caught her attention reminding her that she had more important things going on right now. She squeezed back, and felt a rush of excitement thinking of the two weeks she was going to spend with Jack in a tropical paradise.

She took one more quick look out the window and decided a new bakery across the street wasn't that important. She had better things to focus on ... at least for now.

The End.

***

Want to read about more of Lexy's and Nans' adventures? Get the rest of the Lexy Baker series for you iPad:

Killer Cupcakes
Dying For Danish
Murder, Money & Marzipan
3 Bodies and a Biscotti
Bodies, Brownies & Bad Guys
Bake, Battle & Roll

A Note From The Author

Thanks so much for reading my cozy mystery "*Wedded Blintz*". I hope you liked reading it as much as I loved writing it. If you did, and feel inclined to leave a review over at Amazon, I really would appreciate it.

This is book seven of the Lexy Baker series, you can find the rest of the books on my website, or over at Amazon if you want to read more of Lexy's and Nans's adventures.

Also, if you like cozy mysteries, you might like my book "*Dead Wrong*" which is book one in the Blackmoore Sisters series. Set in the seaside town of Noquitt Maine, the Blackmoore sisters will take you on a journey of secrets, romance and maybe even a little magic. I have an excerpt from it at the end of this book.

This book has been through many edits with several people and even some software programs, but since nothing is infallible (even the software programs) you might catch a spelling error or mistake and, if you do, I sure would appreciate it if you let me know - you can contact me at lee@leighanndobbs.com.

Oh, and I love to connect with my readers so please do visit me on facebook at http://

www.facebook.com/leighanndobbsbooks or at my website http://www.leighanndobbs.com.

Are you signed up to get notifications of my latest releases and special contests? Go to: http://www.leighanndobbs.com/newsletter and enter your email address to signup - I promise never to share it and I only send emails every couple of weeks so I won't fill up your inbox.

About The Author

Leighann Dobbs discovered her passion for writing after a twenty year career as a software engineer. She lives in New Hampshire with her husband Bruce, their trusty Chihuahua mix Mojo and beautiful rescue cat, Kitty. When she's not reading, gardening or selling antiques, she likes to write romance and cozy mystery novels and novelettes which are perfect for the busy person on the go.

Find out about her latest books and how to get discounts on them by signing up at:

http://www.leighanndobbs.com/newsletter

Connect with Leighann on Facebook and Twitter

http://facebook.com/leighanndobbsbooks

http://twitter.com/leighanndobbs

Other Works By Leighann Dobbs

Lexy Baker
Cozy Mystery Series
* * *

Killer Cupcakes
Dying For Danish
Murder, Money & Marzipan
3 Bodies and a Biscotti
Bodies, Brownies & Bad Guys
Bake, Battle & Roll

Blackmoore Sisters
Cozy Mystery Series
* * *

Dead Wrong
Dead & Buried
Dead Tide

Contemporary
Romance
* * *

Reluctant Romance
Sweet Escapes - 4 Romance stories in one book

Dobbs "Fancytales"
Regency Romance Fairytales Series
* * *

Something In Red
Snow White and the Seven Rogues
Dancing on Glass
The Beast of Edenmaine

***

Excerpt From Dead Wrong:

Morgan Blackmoore tapped her finger lightly on the counter, her mind barely registering the low buzz of voices behind her in the crowded coffee shop as she mentally prioritized the tasks that awaited her back at her own store.

"Here you go, one yerba mate tea and a vanilla latte." Felicity rang up the purchase, as Morgan dug in the front pocket of her faded denim jeans for some cash which she traded for the two paper cups.

Inhaling the spicy aroma of the tea, she turned to leave, her long, silky black hair swinging behind her. Elbowing her way through the crowd, she headed toward the door. At this time of morning, the coffee shop was filled with locals and Morgan knew almost all of them well enough to exchange a quick greeting or nod.

Suddenly a short, stout figure appeared, blocking her path. Morgan let out a sharp breath, recognizing the figure as Prudence Littlefield.

Prudence had a long running feud with the Blackmoore's which dated back to some sort of run-in she'd had with Morgan's grandmother when they were young girls. As a result, Prudence loved to harass and berate the Blackmoore girls in public.

Morgan's eyes darted around the room, looking for an escape route.

"Just who do you think you are?" Prudence demanded, her hands fisted on her hips, legs spaced shoulder width apart. Morgan noticed she was wearing her usual knee high rubber boots and an orange sunflower scarf.

Morgan's brow furrowed over her ice blue eyes as she stared at the older woman's prune like face.

"Excuse me?"

"Don't you play dumb with me Morgan Blackmoore. What kind of concoction did you give my Ed? He's been acting plumb crazy."

Morgan thought back over the previous week's customers. Ed Littlefield *had* come into her herbal remedies shop, but she'd be damned if she'd announce to the whole town what he was after.

She narrowed her eyes at Prudence. "That's between me and Ed."

Prudence's cheeks turned crimson. Her nostrils flared. "You know what *I* think," she said narrowing her eyes and leaning in toward Morgan, "I think you're a witch, just like your great-great-great-grandmother!"

Morgan felt an angry heat course through her veins. There was nothing she hated more than being called a witch. She was a Doctor of

Pharmacology with a Master Herbalist's license, not some sort of spell-casting conjurer.

The coffee shop had grown silent. Morgan could feel the crowd staring at her. She leaned forward, looking wrinkled old Prudence Littlefield straight in the eye.

"Well now, I think we know that's not true," she said, her voice barely above a whisper, "Because if I was a witch, I'd have turned you into a newt long ago."

Then she pushed her way past the old crone and fled out the coffee shop door.

***

Fiona Blackmoore stared at the amethyst crystal in front of her wondering how to work it into a pendant. On most days, she could easily figure out exactly how to cut and position the stone, but right now her brain was in a pre-caffeine fog.

Where was Morgan with her latte?

She sighed, looking at her watch. It was ten past eight, Morgan should be here by now, she thought impatiently.

Fiona looked around the small shop, *Sticks and Stones*, she shared with her sister. An old cottage that had been in the family for generations, it sat at one of the highest points in their town of Noquitt, Maine.

Turning in her chair, she looked out the back window. In between the tree trunks that made up a small patch of woods, she had a bird's eye view of the sparkling, sapphire blue Atlantic Ocean in the distance.

The cottage sat about 500 feet inland at the top of a high cliff that plunged into the Atlantic. If the woods were cleared, like the developers wanted, the view would be even better. But Fiona would have none of that, no matter how much the developers offered them, or how much they needed the money. She and her sisters would never sell the cottage.

She turned away from the window and surveyed the inside of the shop. One side was setup as an apothecary of sorts. Antique slotted shelves loaded with various herbs lined the walls. Dried weeds hung from the rafters and several mortar and pestles stood on the counter, ready for whatever herbal concoctions her sister was hired to make.

On her side sat a variety of gemologist tools and a large assortment of crystals. Three antique oak and glass jewelry cases displayed her creations. Fiona smiled as she looked at them. Since childhood she had been fascinated with rocks and gems so it was no surprise to anyone when she grew up to become a gemologist and jewelry designer, creating jewelry not only for its beauty, but also for its healing properties.

The two sisters vocations suited each other perfectly and they often worked together providing customers with crystal and herbal healing for whatever ailed them.

The jangling of the bell over the door brought her attention to the front of the shop. She breathed a sigh of relief when Morgan burst through the door, her cheeks flushed, holding two steaming paper cups.

"What's the matter?" Fiona held her hand out, accepting the drink gratefully. Peeling back the plastic tab, she inhaled the sweet vanilla scent of the latte.

"I just had a run in with Prudence Littlefield!" Morgan's eyes flashed with anger.

"Oh? I saw her walking down Shore road this morning wearing that god-awful orange sunflower scarf. What was the run-in about this time?" Fiona took the first sip of her latte, closing her eyes and waiting for the caffeine to power her blood stream. She'd had her own run-ins with Pru Littlefield and had learned to take them in stride.

"She was upset about an herbal mix I made for Ed. She called me a witch!"

"What did you make for him?"

"Just some Ginkgo, Ginseng and Horny Goat Weed ... although the latter he said was for Prudence."

Fiona's eyes grew wide. "Aren't those herbs for impotence?"

Morgan shrugged "Well, that's what he wanted."

"No wonder Prudence was mad...although you'd think just being married to her would have caused the impotence."

Morgan burst out laughing. "No kidding. I had to question his sanity when he asked me for it. I thought maybe he had a girlfriend on the side."

Fiona shook her head trying to clear the unwanted images of Ed and Prudence Littlefield together.

"Well, I wouldn't let it ruin my day. You know how *she* is."

Morgan put her tea on the counter, then turned to her apothecary shelf and picked several herbs out of the slots. "I know, but she always seems to know how to push my buttons. Especially when she calls me a witch."

Fiona grimaced. "Right, well I wish we *were* witches. Then we could just conjure up some money and not be scrambling to pay the taxes on this shop and the house."

Morgan sat in a tall chair behind the counter and proceeded to measure dried herbs into a mortar.

"I know. I saw Eli Stark in town yesterday and he was pestering me about selling the shop again."

"What did you tell him?"

"I told him we'd sell over our dead bodies." Morgan picked up a pestle and started grinding away at the herbs.

Fiona smiled. Eli Stark had been after them for almost a year to sell the small piece of land their shop sat on. He had visions of buying it, along with some adjacent lots in order to develop the area into high end condos.

Even though their parents early deaths had left Fiona, Morgan and their two other sisters property rich but cash poor the four of them agreed they would never sell. Both the small shop and the stately ocean home they lived in had been in the family for generations and they didn't want *their* generation to be the one that lost them.

The only problem was, although they owned the properties outright, the taxes were astronomical and, on their meager earnings, they were all just scraping by to make ends meet.

All the more reason to get this necklace finished so I can get paid. Thankfully, the caffeine had finally cleared the cobwebs in her head and Fiona was ready to get to work. Staring down at the amethyst, a vision of the perfect shape to cut the stone appeared in her mind. She grabbed her tools and started shaping the stone.

Fiona and Morgan were both lost in their work. They worked silently, the only sounds in the little shop being the scrape of mortar on pestle and the hum of Fiona's gem grinding tool mixed with a few melodic tweets and chirps that floated in from the open window.

Fiona didn't know how long they were working like that when the bell over the shop door chimed again. She figured it must have been an hour or two judging by the fact that the few sips left in the bottom of her latte cup had grown cold.

She smiled, looking up from her work to greet their potential customer, but the smile froze on her face when she saw who it was.

Sheriff Overton stood in the door flanked by two police officers. A toothpick jutted out of the side of Overton's mouth and judging by the looks on all three of their faces, they weren't there to buy herbs or crystals.

Fiona could almost hear her heart beating in the silence as the men stood there, adjusting their eyes to the light and getting their bearings.

"Can we help you?" Morgan asked, stopping her work to wipe her hands on a towel.

Overton's head swiveled in her direction like a hawk spying a rabbit in a field.

"That's her." He nodded to the two uniformed men who approached Morgan hesitantly. Fiona recognized one of the men as Brody Hunter, whose older brother Morgan had dated all through high school. She saw Brody look questioningly at the Sheriff.

The other man stood a head taller than Brody. Fiona noticed his dark hair and broad shoulders but her assessment of him stopped there when she saw him pulling out a pair of handcuffs.

Her heart lurched at the look of panic on her sister's face as the men advanced toward her.

"Just what is this all about?" She demanded, standing up and taking a step toward the Sheriff.

There was no love lost between the Sheriff and Fiona. They'd had a few run-ins and she thought he was an egotistical bore and probably crooked too. He ignored her question focusing his attention on Morgan. The next words out of his mouth chilled Fiona to the core.

"Morgan Blackmoore ... you're under arrest for the murder of Prudence Littlefield."

53907258R00119

Made in the USA
Lexington, KY
24 July 2016

Made in the USA
Columbia, SC
21 July 2021